How to Please a Princely Fae

COZY MONSTER ROMANCE

WILD OAK WOODS
BOOK THREE

JANUARY BELL

HOW TO PLEASE A PRINCELY FAE

Cover by Book Brander Boutique, illustration by Kateryna www.romancepremades.com

Published by January Bell

www.januarybellromance.com

Copyright © 2024 January Bell

This is a work of fiction. Unless otherwise indicated, all the names, characters, businesses, places, events and incidents in this book are either the product of the author's imagination or used in a fictitious manner. Any resemblance to actual persons, living or dead, or actual events is purely coincidental.

All rights reserved. No portion of this book may be reproduced in any form without permission from the publisher, except as permitted by U.S. copyright law. For permissions contact: admin@januarybellromance.com

For sub-rights inquiries, please contact Jessica Watterson at Sandra Djikstra Literary Agency.

❦ Created with Vellum

CHAPTER 1

WILLOW

The greenhouse has always been my favorite place. Ever since I was a young witch, new to the world, new to magic, new to Wild Oak Woods, the greenhouse has been my refuge.

In here, the world outside fades away behind the thick glass panes.

Whether snow banked on the outside of the walls, melting and refreezing in icy sheets from the warmth within, or garish autumn leaves piled outside, crunchy and crisp, or the last gasps of cold in spring, or the relentless heat of summer in the woods—the greenhouse is the same.

Green. So many shades of green. The grayish-green of the moss tucked into planters of more finicky tropical denizens of the greenhouse, whose deep viridian glossy leaves spread like fans overhead. The emerald and ruby splotched leaves of the coleus, the deep purple green of the rosemallow, the variegated lime of the hostas.

I don't need to close my eyes to escape here.

The greenhouse is a world unto itself.

Every plant has a name and a purpose, and there is special comfort in knowing each and every last one.

As the local apothecary and resident potion brewer of Wild Oak Woods, I had better.

I run my hands over the tender new leaves of the tray of medicinal seedlings, murmuring their names under my breath.

"Fenugreek, basil, turmeric, mint, coriander, chamomile, calendula, hyssop, echinacea, feverfew, goldenseal..."

It soothes me.

I need soothing after this evening.

My molars grind together, and I immediately pull my hand back from the fresh leaves, not wishing to taint them with the foul mood I can't seem to get under control.

The foul mood that's pestered me since a very specific day.

The day Kieran came to my shop.

Kieran.

I've become used to the longing that bubbles to the surface when I think of him, the bubble that bursts nearly as soon as it encounters the stark difference in how I would like him to feel about me... and how he very clearly does.

I pluck a sprig of mint before I have a chance to even realize what I'm doing, rubbing it between my fingers and releasing that unmistakably crisp aroma. A sheen of sweat coats my fingers, the warmth of the greenhouse so at odds with the outside chill that the thick fabric of my nicest dress is much, much too hot.

A long exhalation passes through my parted lips and I choke back a sob, feeling stupid, so stupid, for having put on my nicest things tonight for the town's festival.

A festival that went so poorly—beyond poorly, really—that my own personal grievances should be the least of my concerns.

I should be concerned with the fact that not one, but three— three!—of some sort of Elder Gods appeared at the festival, demanding brides from my own coven of witches... or else.

Or else what, I have no idea.

The mint falls to the floor in a spent clump of green, but its essence clings to my hands and I bring them to my face, inhaling deeply.

And begin to sob. Not the sweet, pretty weeping I've seen some other women do, a feat that astonishes me more than any magic; no, this is ugly, wracking crying, and completely, utterly selfish.

Finally, I sink to the large flagstones that line the greenhouse floor, sniffling and spent.

Selfish. That's what I am.

Three Elder Gods have demanded wives from our village, for what purpose, I have no idea—and yet all I can think of is how I should volunteer.

Not to save another, no, but to get away from Kieran.

Kieran, who has made clear that not only is he not interested in me, but that he doesn't even like me.

Kieran, who I've spent more time pining over than is in any way appropriate.

Kieran, who could care less if I'd done as the duchess did and threw myself at one of the gods and vanished into thin air.

So I said I might as well agree to marry one of them.

And then, like any good, dramatic witch, I fled the scene of the festival and sought refuge and quiet in my greenhouse.

The plants are all leaning in, the way they do when I have strong emotions, trying to comfort me.

It just makes me feel guilty.

Guilty and stupid for taking time on my appearance tonight, in hopes that Kieran might finally see me. See me, and realize I've been waiting for him and wanting him since the moment he awkwardly stepped over the threshold of my apothecary several weeks ago.

His pretty purple skin, the iridescent, breath-taking green of his beetle wings, and the small deer's horns that protrude from his head—all of that was striking as could be, just as his face is the most elegant and refined I've ever seen.

He's ridiculously beautiful.

The bashful fae that offered to assist me, an offer I took up immediately, has been nowhere to be seen since that first day. The first day, during which I immediately and stupidly fell head over heels for him. Kieran had followed me around like a little lost puppy dog, all earnestness and eagerness to please, thoughtful and receptive to my instructions, and that first day, I thought I must have truly been the luckiest witch in all the wild woods to have him walk through my door, the perfect assistant.

But now he is ridiculously cold under all that beauty; none of the warmth and excitement I thought I saw in him exists anymore, if it ever did at all.

"I don't know what changed," I wail, curling up into my knees, rubbing my eyes against the fabric of my skirts.

A leaf from the tropical laurel tree, my prize specimen, slowly tickles the back of my neck, a gesture of solidarity and caring.

It stands in the middle of the greenhouse, limbs carefully and painstakingly trimmed to still allow as much sunlight in as possible, though the darkness it casts helps shelter some of my shade-loving plants. The laurel was planted by my father, a green witch who taught me just how to harvest its inner bark for cinnamon, as well as the spell to heal it immediately after.

I place a palm on the trunk, and the leaves above make a gentle, soothing susurrus.

I don't know what to think about the appearance of the old magic beings at the festival.

I sniff and brush the last of my tears away with the back of my hand, then hold onto the laurel tree as I pull myself upright.

One thing's for sure—I need to put away my childish attachment and hurt for Kieran or I might as well take up their offer and marry one of them, if only to be rid of my unrequited feelings for him.

I breathe in, the cinnamon scent of the trunk filling my nose, and I lean my forehead against the tree, feeling the life in it, the gentleness of its spirit.

My jaw unclenches, my shoulders loosen, and exhaustion begins to take the place of my silly sorrow.

Tonight, I will sleep.

Tomorrow, I will make a plan: either marry one of the mysterious Elder Gods that appeared and leave the Wild Oak Woods, or stay here and put Kieran fully out of my mind.

A sigh slips out of me and I take a stuttering breath, my lungs apparently spent from crying.

I know which of the two will be easier.

A rare xëchno plant sits on the table nearest the laurel. A single massive violet bud droops from the yellow-tinged leaves.

I frown at it, because no matter what I've done to coax the bud into finally blooming, the plant just gets sicker and sicker. No spell has worked, no charmed water or carefully concocted fertilizer has done the trick.

It makes me sadder, and that hollow pit of gloom widens a bit more.

I brush my fingertips across the petal-soft bud, and my eyebrows shoot up as motes of light glisten in their wake.

"I wish I knew how to help you," I tell the xëchno plant. Impulsively, I add, "I wish I could forget Kieran, too."

I watch the plant for a moment, so sure I felt a whisper of magic from it, or perhaps from me, after all, but my hopes are dashed as the bud stays tightly closed, the leaves as yellow-green and sad as ever.

"Goodnight, little plant," I murmur, headed for bed.

I have all the plant and potion magic knowledge I can stuff inside my brain, and still I know there's no better remedy for a hurt of the heart like a good night's sleep.

CHAPTER 2

KIERAN

I storm into the apothecary, ready to tear the store apart and make that absolute minx of a little witch listen to reason. How dare she offer to take some washed-up ancient god's hand in marriage? How dare she be so careless with herself?

Doesn't she know she is *everything*?

My fangs pierce my bottom lip as I grind my teeth. My nostrils flare, and my heart pounds so hard it fairly tries to escape the cage of my ribs.

How dare Willow even think about endangering herself? Of giving up everything it's so clear she loves in order to meet the extremely cliché demands of some ancient magic being?

Absolutely *not*.

I am a prince of the Unseelie Underhill, and I will not allow it.

My nose scrunches and my grimace deepens because that title is a double-edged sword, primed to cut both ways.

I am a prince of the Unseelie Underhill, and Willow deserves so much more than I can give her. I am a creature of darkness, spawn of an Unseelie queen who would kill me if I so much as deigned to breathe the air of the Underhill again.

Willow does not deserve to be yoked to me.

I should have walked away from this job and her the moment I realized what a treasure of a witch she was, but all the reasons that keep me away from her are the same reasons that I haven't left.

I am selfish and callous, through and through.

Somewhere in the dark, a cricket chirps, singing a song to itself and jolting me from my thoughts. I see well in the dark, as do all things raised in the Underhill, and it takes me no time at all to deduce the cricket and I are alone.

"Willow?" I call out, just in case.

She's not here, not in the store itself, though I hardly expected her to be here. The floorboards creak under my feet as I walk through the winding shelves and displays that I now know by heart.

There is the feverfew potion she brewed only yesterday, bottled in tiny glass jars and sealed with magic and tied with a velvet ribbon. A hand-lettered tag swings gently as I walk by.

For fevers and headaches, it reads.

It won't work on the headache I have.

My hands ball into fists, feckless and incapable as always, because those... beings that appeared tonight won't be beaten by measly physical violence.

Though I would do my best if I had the chance to try.

Ga'Rek would laugh at the thought, were he here to hear it. The huge orc's spent most of my life trying and failing to teach me to fight, to stand up for myself.

Of course, the one time I took a lesson of self-defense and applied it, I was banished from the Underhill along with my two companions. My only two friends, though I'm not sure they feel the same about me or if I'm just some unfortunate responsibility they've been saddled with since I was born.

I know everyone else feels that way about me. My mother, the Dark Queen, certainly did. I'm sure she was thrilled to wash her elegant hands of me the moment I protected myself and gave her an excuse to. I was never the heir. I wasn't even the spare.

No one's ever wanted me.

My mood is positively foul as I round the corner into what Willow calls her laboratory. The room reeks of magic, so many powerful incantations and charms worked here over the years that their imprint might never be truly washed away.

It smells of Willow, too.

She's not here, and that bothers me.

The longer I spend time with her, the more used to her moods I grow. When she's thoughtful or bothered by a problem a customer brings her, she's in here, in her green-lit laboratory, surrounded by her potion-making ingredients, her beautiful scarlet-red hair curling in the heat and humidity over her cast-iron cauldron.

A cauldron she named Fred, because of course she did.

A small smile lifts the corner of one lip, but the fire beneath Fred remains dark.

There is no Willow here, and the magical signature of her laboratory seems even more profound without the curvy beauty.

She is small and soft, but her magic packs as much of a punch as anyone I've ever met.

A surprising sense of pride wells in me for the witch.

Pride I have no place to feel, seeing as how I have nothing to do with it.

The only thing I will cause the witch is trouble, just as I have always done. Shame and anger curdle under my skin, the familiar feeling of revulsion making my wings twitch as I walk towards the greenhouse.

It's Willow's favorite place, everything about her softening further the longer she spends in here.

Often, I find myself drawn to her and her magic as she works in the greenhouse, the scent of the green witch's charms somehow triggering a deep response within me.

I pause in the doorway, the heat and humidity of the room seeping into my skin, expecting to find the lush-bodied witch within.

I can almost envision her just there, behind a massive cream-colored bloom with her eyes nearly closed. Her curly red hair drifting over her shoulders, one of her sleeves almost always falling down her arm, her skin as creamy as the bloom itself—a flower I've never noticed before tonight.

My feet take another step into the greenhouse, almost moving of their own accord. "Willow," I call but there's no answer. It's clear she's not here but that's not the only thing that's different. A humid air is moist, heavy almost, and there's a scent of magic hanging on it.

There's a spicy tang to it, and it's like nothing I recognize.

It's closer to my mother's magic the Dark Queen of the Unseelie fae than to anything I've become accustomed to Willow using. Still, it doesn't have the slippery feel of my mother's magic, and though it's not hers, it leaves me wary of it all the same.

Some kind of spell work has happened here.

I don't know what kind. I was never taught enough about magic to be able to discern between the spell work, only I was raised around enough of it to know that something has been cast.

My boots tap against the floor, a low thrum of power washing over me. It's pulling me forward, further into the greenhouse, distracting me from my task of finding Willow.

"Willow," I breathe.

I should be looking for Willow; I need to know if she is okay. I need to know if she's truly thinking of going off with some foul creature that just happened to appear at the fall festival. It seems quite a sudden decision to make this evening.

I need to know if she is leaving.

Magic is whispering to me. I don't know what it's saying, but it's asking a question. A question I feel the need to answer.

"I shouldn't want her," I state out loud, almost startling at the sound of my own voice. "She deserves more than what I can give her, she deserves to be safe."

A humorless laugh escapes my lips. "I don't even know who I am." I pause, sadness threatening to swallow me up.

I never got a chance to figure out who I *was*, much less who I am now without the Underhill. Without the pressures of being even a spare to the throne, without the malicious gaze of my mother, always expecting me to do something I was never quite sure of for reasons I never understood.

For reasons that now, without her, without all the pressure of the Underhill, weigh on my shoulders—and start to unravel.

In more ways than one.

"I don't deserve someone who is kind, who doesn't have a past that threatens to stab them in the back when they least expect it. She deserves someone without an agenda who can love her in all the ways that she deserves to be loved and in all the ways that I don't know how."

I purse my lips.

The spicy scent of magic increases exponentially and I inhale, wanting to find her and failing at even that small task.

I'm not sure I'll ever be anything but an unwanted spare, a prince that's a problem to be solved, by violence or neglect.

I sink back onto my heels, cradling my head as my thoughts spin like weapons.

Eventually, all I feel is numb, tired, and all too aware of the transparent glass overhead. The stars configured in constellations I'd never seen before I left the Underhill twinkling overhead in the black night sky.

Even the plants seem greener here, which is no surprise considering all the care and attention Willow gives them. She's more of a mother to every living thing in this greenhouse than my own mother ever was to me.

I can practically hear Caelan's laugh echoing in my ear.

"Poor little prince," he would coo.

There would be no shortage of derision in his words, no matter the truth in mine.

"Sometimes I wish I could forget," I say out loud. "I wish I could start fresh." My fingers reach for the creamy bloom in front of me, and I luxuriate in the velvet feel of the petals. "Sometimes I wish I could be who I want to be instead of who I've been made to be."

A bolt of energy courses through my fingertips, I drop the petal as though it is at fault. It is ridiculous, of course, no flower is capable of that type of magical charge.

My lips curl in a half smile, and I force a reluctant laugh at my own wild imagination. Alas, it's quickly cut off by the reminder that I need to find Willow and make sure she's not about to walk into the forest to do something we will both regret for the rest of our lives.

I clench my teeth. I know a thing or two about regret.

Exhaustion slips over me, replacing some of the chaotic worry that has had me in its grip since the beings first arrived at the autumn festival. Certainly, even the sometimes tempestuous Willow has not decided to do something so foolhardy as to take them up on their offer.

Sure, she loses her temper when her potions don't go the way she's planned, or when an experiment doesn't pan out the way she wishes, but I have never once seen her lose her patience with anything or anyone else in the store or in the entire town of Wild Oak Woods. It's more than I can say for myself, or Caelan, and probably even Ga'Rek.

She's a good woman. Powerful, beautiful, full-bodied. There's a simple shyness about her in spite of all of this, but it only adds to the air of mystery around her. I glide from the greenhouse, my footfalls now near silent on the flooring. Whatever's hung heavy in the air has at least done the job setting someone at ease. I pass by the large wooden desk were Willow's taught me to wrap up her potions and unguents, to inventory the plants and herbs and tools that she uses in her apothecary. I open the door hidden by a bookcase behind the desk and enter into Willow's private residence.

I pause, nearly overwhelmed with dizziness at the strength of her scent lingering in these halls. The halls, like the rest of her home and shop, are alive with color. Sweeping greens the likes of which I'd never seen in the Underhill threaten to overtake every other shade in the rainbow here. I follow the herbal scent I've grown so accustomed to associating with her I doubt I can ever smell it without envisioning her.

I find myself in front of a slightly ajar door I shouldn't go through. She has sought privacy, I should be willing to give it to her. Then I remember the way the gods of the Elder Forest descended upon the quaint festival and laid claim to three witches from Wild Oak Woods. I decide that it's more important to respect her safety and ensure she's not giving herself up to them than it is to abide by a rule of privacy that wouldn't even apply to a door already open.

Probably.

I step over the threshold, and there she is: her mouth slightly open. Lips full and slow, asleep, her eyes red-tinged as though she's been crying. Indeed, a shining rivulet winds from the the corner of nose, one last drop quivering and falling to the ivory pillow.

It's an ivory that doesn't even begin to compare to the pale luster of her alabaster skin and the delicious autumnal red of her hair falling in curls over her cheek. They tumble over the smooth column of her neck and her lush round breasts, which have driven me to distraction over the past weeks.

I hardly know what I'm doing. My feet and body move of their own accord. All I know is that I need to be near her and that she has overpowered all of my good sense.

CHAPTER 3

WILLOW

My eyes squeeze shut, and I burrow deeper under my heavy blanket. Every cell in my body resists the fact that it's morning.

My head still hurts from crying, and I know when I look in the mirror later, my eyes will be disgustingly swollen. I'll have to slap some salve on them and hope that my skin underneath isn't peeling.

Ah, the endless joys of sensitive skin. Fairest of them all? More like the fucking itchiest of them all.

I'm in a horrible mood.

I want to pretend daylight isn't streaming through the stained-glass window.

At least it's pretty when it sends color all through my room. Still, I don't open my eyes.

I installed it when I made this room my own seven years ago. It was quite an undertaking. The stained-glass window's in the image of the summer rose in full bloom, one of my favorite flowers and one of the hardest to grow, captured in a state of eternal perfection.

I know if I look, the deep crimson of the petals will have turned a lighter shade of pink, the way they always do in the morning. The green glow of the leaves and stem will be reflected all over my pale cream-colored bedding.

It's a welcome splash of my favorite colors.

And yet.

I don't want to get up.

I don't want to open my swollen, sore eyes.

And I don't want to accept any of the things that have happened over the past few weeks are real.

My hands fist in the bedsheets and I point my feet, unable to stop my teensy morning stretch.

I only want to live my little life in quiet and in peace the way I have for as long as I can remember.

I wish to remain untroubled and unbothered by a certain lavender-skinned fae prince who has occupied too much of my mind, too much of my heart, and too much of my attention.

I roll to the side, knowing I'm putting off the inevitable, and then stop.

My bed is warmer than it should be.

Why is my bed... hot?

I finally force my eyes open when I hear my owl familiar hoot gently from his perch on the inside of the door.

Sure enough, Chirp's great brown eyes are fixed squarely on my face, and he hoots again, a soft sound. A soft sound that, though I might be used to it, I am extremely alarmed by because Chirp knows better than to make any sound at all when I'm still in bed.

The reason for the warmth and the hoots suddenly becomes absurdly and overwhelmingly obvious.

I suck in a shocked breath, my heart hammering in my chest.

A certain lavender-skinned fae lies next to me.

Kieran is in my bed. The tinted light from the window makes him look even more ethereal, even more handsome than even I could have thought possible. It caresses the delicious slope of his cheekbones, greens and pinks playing across his angular jaw and soaking into his silvery hair.

What a way to wake up.

I can't seem to stop staring at him. What am I supposed to do now?

The sheet slips down his shoulder, exposing the lean muscle of his biceps. They are much larger than I would've imagined under his clothes... and I have imagined them quite often.

Wait. *Wait*. My eyes, even in their swollen state, somehow to manage to widen even more.

Where... where is his shirt?

Why is Kieran in my bed?

Why is Kieran *naked* in my bed?

What is happening?!

Still as a statue, I replay last night's events in my head, confused and at a complete loss.

There are a few facts to consider here.

One, Kieran has made it immensely clear that he dislikes me intensely. He hardly responds to anything I say. All of my attempts at idle chitchat and overtures of friendship have been completely rebuffed.

Two, that behavior is the complete opposite of how we spent our first few days together. My throat tightens at the painful juxtaposition.

When he began working with me, he was easy to talk to. Warm. A good listener, in addition to his good looks.

Someone easy to like, someone even easier to pine after.

But since then?

Kieran's been anything but pleasant. I thought I could draw him out with smiles and small talk. But every attempt has been met with stony silence and a cold shoulder.

Shoulders I've stared at much too long, pining over them, which are now naked next to me in my bed for reasons that are completely beyond my comprehension.

I'm afraid to move, because what if it's not just his shoulders and arms that are naked? What if there's more nakedness under the sheets?

What if he is *completely* naked?

Then the worst thought yet...

What if this is all some great prank?

Fresh tears prick behind my eyes, and my lip begins to wobble as I stare at the beautiful male in my bed.

I wouldn't put it past Caelan. Caelan, a well-known trickster, easily could have put him up to this. Wren, my coven sister and his mate, wouldn't be so cruel, though, to allow this... would she?

What if everyone has somehow conspired against me and my ridiculous crush on the fae male who can't stand me?

A tear squeezes out of my eye, and I'm too scared of waking him to wipe it away.

Perhaps this is part of some coven plan to make sure *I* go to the Elder Gods and volunteer to be one of their demanded witch brides. Unhappiness crashes over me, a tempestuous wave, one I'm not strong enough to resist.

I'm afraid to breathe. I'm afraid to move.

I'm terrified to wake him up and find out the answers to the questions that rush through my head, a flood threatening to drown me.

Kieran, however, saves me from my own downward spiral.

Because he moves first.

His arm slides over my waist, warm and strong, as he snuggles closer, pulling me tight.

I freeze.

I don't dare breathe.

A shiver goes through me at his proximity—*his touch*—and the reality of having him in my bed, and I'm chilled to the bone despite the heat from his beautiful body. A body I have no business thinking about, a body that does not belong in my bed whatsoever, and yet, a body that is now wrapping itself around me, causing my heart to palpitate.

Maybe I should take something for that.

I'm sure I have something for heart palpitations in my stock of apothecary herbs.

I stare at the ceiling, frozen, pinned under his arm.

There is a slight water stain that resembles a Luna moth, likely due to some leak in the roof that I haven't had the time or inclination or know-how to fix. I wonder if it will take flight if I blink at it in shock enough.

Maybe there's a potion I can take to inoculate myself against the desire and longing and fear that ripple through me, more powerful than anything I have felt in my entire life.

A life I'm starting to think was lovely and safe *without* a gorgeous fae male in bed with me.

The sheet slides off the rest of him as he moves, and my curiosity is satisfied.

I shouldn't look.

But there it is, the stark-naked proof that he is very much bare on bottom.

He drapes a heavy thigh over my legs possessively, another arm snaking under my head, and it's everything I can do to stay quiet and stay still as I try to figure out how to extricate myself from a predicament I've been wanting to happen for weeks.

Be careful what you wish for.

I grit my teeth together.

There must be a way to get out of this that won't embarrass us both.

I squeeze my eyes shut, stupefied by the turn of events and completely at a loss for how to navigate them.

If this is some trick by my sister witches, it is a cruel one.

Maybe I should think harder on going to the Elder Gods if *this* is how they think of me.

Although, if Wren or anyone else in the coven is behind this, I'm not so sure I want to save them from whatever the Elder Gods consider coming.

It's a mean thought, and I regret it immediately and decide I need to get over it and do something about this.

I inhale deeply, then hold my breath as I try to wriggle away from Kieran with the last bits of my dignity intact.

A feat which would truly be something, considering all of his very large and impressive intactness is pressing up against me.

All of my lackluster attempts to get away from the purple fae, however, prove fruitless as his face nuzzles against my shoulder, shocking me into stillness once more.

"Well, well, well," his purring voice says, tickling against my skin. The arm around my waist pulls me in even tighter than before, until I'm wedged into his perfectly sculpted and still very naked chest. "What do we have here?"

I suck in a breath and press my palm against his chest, wriggling to get free.

And immediately decide that his excited response to that effort is working against me.

"I've had enough." I push against him again, scowling. "If this is a joke, it's a cruel one, and I'm not going to play nice any longer. What do you mean, *what do we have here?*" I snarl, sounding nothing like myself. "*You* are the one who crawled into my bed naked and are now holding me tight, *naked*, in my own bed, and did I mention you're *naked?*"

"Well," Kieran says, and there's a hint of reproach in his voice that takes me aback.

As if this situation is my fault!

"The only problem I see with any of this is that I'm the only one who's naked," he continues.

There's no hint of humor, no hint of anything but heat.

Something is wrong.

"What is going on with you?" I ask, startled out of my own self-loathing and self-pity by his completely unbothered demeanor.

Well, judging by the way his cock twitches against my thigh, that part is very much bothered, but not in the way it should be.

Unbothered is not a word I thought I would ever use to describe Kieran.

Kieran's natural state is bothered.

Bothered is, in fact, the adjective that describes him best. I can't think of one time since he turned cold when he *hasn't* seemed bothered. Put out. Disdainful.

I try to form a coherent sentence. Try and fail.

His cock is very distracting in its earnest waggling, and I get the feeling he's making it jump against my skin to see what I'll do.

I wrinkle my nose, because what the actual hells is going on?

"You can't come into my bed naked and then make jokes about it like this is normal behavior," I tell him.

"Well." He draws the word out long. A bevy of tiny expressions flurries across his face: shock, hurt, surprise, and maybe even confusion.

I've never seen any of them before. No, the fae champion of disdain only does ice.

Never confusion.

Definitely not hurt.

"Now," I say, mustering courage I didn't know I had. "Either you tell me exactly what is going on here, or you can't come back to work for me again."

I didn't expect to make the ultimatum.

The moment it flies past my lips, I feel that perhaps I've gone too far. For one, I do enjoy having the help, and secondly, Kieran looks so confused by the turn of events that alarms begin to blare in earnest in my head.

Well, clearly, something is amiss.

Something is very amiss indeed, considering Kieran is *naked* in my bed.

Things are not exactly what they seem.

An observation that helps not at all, thank you, witchy prescience.

"Well, I wish I could tell you what was going on," Kieran says slowly, the words stilted. Now *this* is the Kieran I recognize. These mannerisms are much closer to what I'm used to than the delighted, whimsical tone he used on waking.

I stammer out a garbled nonsense word as his statement lands in my brain.

He doesn't know why he's naked in my bed?

"Did you have too much to drink? Are you on some kind of mushroom?"

His eyebrows arch so high they nearly disappear into the beautiful silvery hair falling from his head again, another expression I haven't seen on his face before now.

"Answer me," I demand, feeling incredibly put upon and sorry for myself. Both feelings are unfamiliar, and I dislike them more intensely the deeper they take root.

He looses an exasperated sigh, and he blinks slowly at me, the cat-like pointed tips of his ears twitching slightly.

His expression changes lightning-fast as he considers me.

Goddess, I wish I'd done something about my swollen eyes. I'm sure I look awful. Not that it matters. Now is not the time to wish I looked good for him, goddess save me from myself.

A strange buzzing sound comes from behind him. Well, the sound isn't strange, but it sure is awkward to hear in my bed.

I've heard it so often now that I know exactly what it is.

His wings are rustling behind him. It's a sign of his high agitation. I've only heard them like that when he was completely confused or flustered by one of our shoppers, or if I've asked him something about his life before he came to Wild Oak Woods.

And now, the noise is a result of being asked why he is, in fact, naked with his cock pressed up against my body.

"I… I… don't know," he finally answers. His gaze dips away from mine before finding it again. "I don't know why I'm in your bed, and I don't even know *who* you are," he says, and this time there is a note of confused longing.

I swallow hard, deciding this is not some cruel joke. In fact, I don't think it is a joke at all.

If it is, he's a victim of it as much as I am.

No, it is becoming increasingly clear that this is a new horrible problem for both of us.

I squint at him.

"You don't know who I am?" I ask, even though he's just said that he doesn't, because what else am I supposed to say?

"Do you know where you are?" I tack it on, thinking as fast as I can. "Do you know your name?" I follow up, since he's failed to answer any of my rapid-fire questions.

"Of course, I know my name," he says, scoffing. "And of course I know where I am." He says, although this time there's a definite uncertainty in the pronunciation.

"Then where are you?" The question is full of trepidation.

Frankly, I don't know what to do with the gorgeous male I've been lusting after for weeks, who doesn't know who he is, or who I am, or, for that matter, where we are.

Or why he's naked in my bed.

In fact, I am one hundred percent sure that I would not know what to do with anyone in this situation.

My heart pounds under my ribs and I take a deep breath, trying to calm myself. Panic never got anyone anywhere. In fact, I grow multiple plants and brew several potions for just this exact feeling, precisely so I can avoid feeling it at all costs.

Me and my customers, of course.

Unfortunately, accessing any of those would require me

somehow getting out of Kieran's iron grip, which just keeps getting tighter.

"Right," I say, as he continues to not answer. "Can you tell me your name?"

"I am Kieran, prince of the Underhill," he says. His nose wrinkles, though, and that hangdog, forlorn expression returns to his face. "Though, I have to admit I'm not sure I know what either of those things mean."

I blow out a breath and slump against my pillow—or where my pillow ought to be, but is just his muscly arm.

There's no doubt in my mind. He isn't acting.

This isn't some cruel joke, and while I'm relieved my coven sisters have not decided to torment me into dedicating myself to or wedding or whatever an Elder God... I'm also terrified of what this means for Kieran.

No one deserves to have their memories taken.

Did the Elder Gods that showed up last night do this? Are they somehow to blame?

Have I somehow painted a target on my back? Have they decided that removing Kieran from my immediate sphere would allow them better access to me or one of the other witches right away?

While a little mean part of me finds that somewhat appealing, because for once it would mean that someone is taking an interest in me romantically... it's also incredibly unappealing. The last thing I want is to end up in some arranged marriage to whatever the hells the Elder Gods are. Logic tells me I don't want to marry anyone who crashes an autumn festival to demand a stranger's hand in marriage.

I sniff. Very uncouth behavior.

Kieran still stares at me, a puppy dog expression firmly in place. He's never looked quite so adorable as he does right now, naked in my bed. Which is a problem, of course it's a problem.

"You can't just get into people's beds naked, Kieran," I tell him.

"I'm not sure how I got here," he says quietly.

Guilt swims through me.

It seems being angry with him would make about as much sense as punishing a Venus fly trap for catching a fly, when it's just in the plant's nature to make a meal of an insect.

"Well," I say, breathing out slowly, trying to control my rampaging thoughts. "Can you start by moving away from me?"

"I'm comfortable," he says, and this time there's no mistaking his arrogance. It shouldn't surprise me, not considering he's an Unseelie fae prince, but it does.

It's as new a behavior quirk as everything else he's done this morning, and I'm realizing I might not know this naked man in my bed at all.

Which, honestly, should be more troubling a thought than it is.

"Get off me," I say, my voice strained.

If he doesn't get off of me soon, I'm fairly sure I will ask him to get off with me, which would be an even bigger problem. It cannot be ethical to ask an amnesiac to satisfy your need for cock.

Something in my tone makes him move. Kieran scoots to the edge of the bed, which only further exposes his perfectly muscled body.

I swallow hard, so loud I'm sure that he can hear it.

Based on the way he smiles down at me, I'm certain he did hear it.

This isn't going well.

"I didn't have to get off of you," he says, "in fact, if you are more comfortable—"

"No," I interrupt, putting my hand directly in his face, "you stay over there. You can't remember why you're here or who I am and," I say, forcing all the patience I have into my voice. "It wouldn't be right for me to take advantage of you."

A slow grin spreads across his face.

Great. I've just fed the cocky ego monster that I didn't know lurked beneath the prince's surface. I didn't know about the monster cock that lurked beneath his pants, either, but that's neither here nor there.

"I think I find that I would like to be taken advantage of," he says.

I bite back a laugh. "There's no time for this," I tell him.

"Why not?" he asks.

"It's still early morning, well, for one," I stutter. I am fully annoyed by this presumptuousness, taken aback by the fact that he seems ready and willing to do everything I've ever dreamed of when it concerns him, and I stumble over my words trying to find a reason why we can't do exactly what we both clearly want to do.

"For one, we have to open the store and get ready to restock the potions for the day," I finally announced.

"Do I work with you?" he asks, looking perplexed.

"You do," I tell him.

"Why?" he asks. "I don't feel like I should be working."

I blow out a breath, both annoyed and somehow amused at our inane predicament. Now that he is further away from me and my brain is working again, I can be amused.

"Well, you do, and you are," I tell him.

"Are we lovers?" he asks, raising an eyebrow. "Is that why you're worried about taking advantage of me in my current state of undress? You are my lover?"

"Excuse me," I say, unduly thrilled and ashamed all at once to hear those words come out of his mouth. "We are not lovers. You are the one that's undressed in my bed—"

"And you're the one that's thinking of taking advantage of me," he interrupts, raising an eyebrow, that cocky half smile back on his face.

Once again, I have to stop myself from laughing. Encouraging this behavior is only going to get us both in a world of trouble.

"You need to put some clothes on," I say in a choked voice.

"What if I like being naked in bed with you?" he says.

I sigh deeply from all the way down in my bones. Arguing with the naked, handsome Kieran who's had a personality transplant along with amnesia overnight is not something I counted on or prepared for in any way, shape or form, especially not the delicious shape of his naked body now fully exposed and lying next to me. I have to avert my eyes. "Do whatever you want," I snap, annoyed. "We need to figure out what happened to you, why you lost your memory, and if the Elder Gods are at all to blame. Plus, we need to do it soon, because I fear the entire Wild Oak Woods is in danger."

"Wild Oak Woods?" he repeats. "Is that where I am?"

"Yes," I say, brightening slightly. "Do you remember it?"

He grins at me and relief rushes through me. If he is remembering already, that's a good sign.

"No," he says, lightly tapping his chin with a finger. "Can't say that I do, but I'm happy to be here."

I roll out of bed and storm over to my cabinet, pulling on clothes and getting dressed as fast as I can. Unfortunately, in my speed, I've forgotten that I have an audience. When I turn back around, lacing up my favorite mauve linen overdress, Kieran's eyes are fixed on me. Devouring me. An unexpected shiver goes up my back.

I've wanted him to look at me like that since the day he came to town and asked to work in my shop. Since the first few days when I thought he was looking at me like that, like I was something delicious to be savored. Like I was a treat he's wanted his whole life and never found his way to. Now he's looking at me like that again completely naked, with a lazy hand around his cock and I don't know what to think.

In fact, I think the sight of him like that has completely ruined my capacity for any thoughts whatsoever and I'm completely sure that there is no draught or magic that could ever wipe the image from my memory.

"I, I, I— You need to put clothes on," I tell him.

"Why?" he asks.

I give him a hard look, because getting used to sassy Kieran is a bad idea. "This isn't the real you," I tell him. I run my hands across my skirt, trying to smooth it out and soothe my feelings at the same time. He would be mortified to know how he is behaving. He blinks, not understanding.

"Because you don't even like me," I tell him coldly, doing my best impression of, well, him. "You don't like me, and you've made that abundantly clear, and it hurts my feelings that you're acting like this now. I don't want to be around you when you," I gesture wildly at him, "look like this." The last sentence is uttered slightly less fervently and a little bit more forlornly. It makes me ashamed when his expression shutters. We stare each other for a long, awkward moment.

"Well, where do you keep my clothes?" he asks.

"You don't sleep here," I say, completely consternated. "You work with me, this isn't your home—this is my home. I don't know where you put your clothes." I turn, walking towards the door, and then practically stumble over the aforementioned clothes. I grunt in annoyance.

"Well, you found them," he says brightly.

I glare, annoyed with him. Unreasonably so, because the poor man is clearly under some sort of spell, and annoyed with myself for being so affected by him. I'm also annoyed with the fact that Kieran is apparently the type of male to leave his clothes in a pile on the floor—truly, a black mark against him.

I begin to bend to pick up the clothes so my unruly houseguest can get them back on his lovely body, only to be beaten to the punch by Kieran himself.

Quick as a flash, he nudges in front of me, stooping to pick up the discarded items and leaving me with the impressive view of his naked rear end. From his perfectly formed derrière, thick with muscle, up to the broad shoulders that I never would have guessed lurked under the drab, loose clothes he prefers. Then, of course, his magnificent wings. They were the first things I noticed about him. They are the most impressive mix of iridescent greens and teals and blues, more beautiful than the stained-glass window I painstakingly chose and installed so many years ago.

Everything about Kieran is beautiful, and I find myself staring openly at him… Three scars across under his gorgeous wings, pale silvery lavender so startling in contrast with his perfection that I can't help myself and I blurt, "What's that?"

"What's what?" he responds. He cranes over one shoulder in an attempt to look at the scars that are now hidden behind the fluttering beauty of his wings.

"You just, you have some…" I stop. It seems unfair to tell a male who can't remember where he comes from that he has scars he can't remember. "Nothing," I say. "Never mind, I just—I'm going to just go get started for the day."

"There's no hurry," he says, that coy note returning to his voice. "You're obviously enjoying looking at me, there's no need to rush off."

I ground myself, caught between annoyance and amusement once again. A playful Kieran is a Kieran I am not equipped to deal with whatsoever. It's much easier to ignore this childish infatuation when the object of my desire would prefer to pretend that I don't exist.

An object of my desire standing naked in my bedroom making cute jokes is a lot harder to ignore.

Chirp the owl hoots softly, winging silently to my shoulder as I cross into the hallway. I suck in a breath and square my shoulders as his claws dig in for balance. I make my way down the hallway of my home to the storefront. I am completely out of sorts. I've never felt this way in my own home. It's always been my sanctuary, the one place where I felt safe. And I'm inordinately and unexpectedly irritated with Kieran for making it a place where I no longer feel that way. It's not fair to him, something has clearly happened to take his memory away.

Whether it's the strange presence from the Elder Forest that made itself known last night, or some other magic… it's best not to get too attached to this version of the fae prince.

I settle in behind the cash wrap, looking over my to-do list that seems to grow longer every day. Chirp wings off into the shop, probably to roost in his favorite sleeping spot amongst the potted asphodel, where he can still look over us as we go about our day. My familiar doesn't like to be too far from the action.

I smile at his soft feathers fondly, grateful for Chirp's steadying presence in such an unsteady time.

I blow out a breath, pushing some of my wayward curls from my face. An unwashed face to go with the uncombed tangle of hair. Heat rises in my cheeks, and I just know I've flushed an entirely unbecoming shade of fuchsia.

I'm so caught up in how unhinged I must look thanks to Kieran's new predicament that I fail to hear him approach.

I stifle my startle, making an awkward noise somewhere between a grunt and a squeak.

Or, perhaps, I simply didn't hear him. As far as I know, he can move like any other fae: soundless, silent, and deadly—something else that he's never shown me he knew how to do until he forgot who he was.

That cocky, handsome grin is in full effect, and I try not to whimper at the sight.

That would be a truly embarrassing sound.

"So, this is where you work?" he asks, looking around with raised brows. "What is it you do?"

"I run an apothecary. This apothecary," I explain gently, waving a hand around the shop. It's hard not to smile at his genuine interest, something I haven't seen from him since the first day he walked through my door.

"You're a healer?" he asks, picking up one of the crystal potion bottles that lines a small display on the counter.

He puts it down carefully, studying the collection of shelves that rise from the solid oak floors.

"No," I tell him, shaking my head and hoping my blush has subsided. "I'm a green witch." I shrug one shoulder. "I'm good with plants. I grow ingredients for healers and sometimes concoct potions for them... but I don't have an affinity for it. All I have an affinity for is growing things."

"A green witch," he repeats, genuine interest all over his face. "I've never met anyone that could do that."

"It's not a common Unseelie talent, from what I know," I tell him. I don't bother to add that he very well may have met another green witch, but he just doesn't remember it. I'm not in the business of casual meanness, and even though Kieran has unwittingly hurt me more times than I can count over the last few weeks, I can't find it in me to return the favor.

"That is very impressive," he says, leaning over to inspect one of the twilight hostas growing in a large planter beside the counter.

"The plant? It's an old—"

"No, you. You're impressive. To be able to grow things and grow them well..." He pauses, now squinting at the rows of cork-topped glass vials and dried ingredients.

I try to see the shop through his eyes, to get a glimpse of whatever has him so entranced, but all I see are shelves that could use a dusting (again), plants that need charmed watering (again) and the fact we're low on lacewing eggs and dragonflies.

"And you do all of this by yourself?" he asks.

The new note of respect in the question nearly makes me preen.

He runs his long purple fingers over the leaves of seedlings I keep on hand to sell as basic spell ingredients.

"You help me, now," I say, biting my lower lip.

He laughs at that, glancing back at me in a way that makes me blush all the way to my scalp. "I have a feeling I have never been much help, and am even less of it now."

There's a self-deprecating sense to his words that I recognize all too well.

Kieran wanders over to where I house the more expensive ingredients, along a much less packed set of cabinets. I can't drag my gaze away from him, though I really should get back to my to-do list.

I scrawl the words "find out what's wrong with Kieran" across the top of my list and glance back up.

He touches a sparkling cut-crystal vase that houses powdered unicorn's horn. Next to it, a glowing phoenix feather rests on a navy velvet pillow, and beside the feather, a brass box full of glittering dragon scales.

"This is really something," he says. "You have quite a collection."

"Ah, thank you," I tell him, feeling pleased despite myself.

I know that he's not in his right mind... but it's nice to be seen.

My throat closes up, and he turns back to the shelves of ingredients and plants and potions.

It's nice to hear someone appreciate the work that I do, and the little shop and little life that I've built for myself. It's not much, and I know it.

An odd emotion sweeps through me, and I cross my arms over my chest, careful not to stain my overdress with the ink quill in my hand.

Being a green witch isn't nearly as flashy or impressive as Nerissa's prognosticating and spell work... or as lucrative as Wren's jewelry-making business. I don't have the incredible people skills that Piper does—in addition to creating some of the best food I've ever eaten, she has an uncanny knack for suggesting exactly the right thing to make someone's day a little brighter.

All I do is grow plants well and make things from them. I'm not particularly good with people, and I certainly won't win any awards for showmanship.

Kieran's clear admiration for my work makes me feel seen in a way I don't think I have felt before. The other witches have never made me feel less than, have never made me feel like anything but one of them. Like a friend. It's not that I need admiration, but it is nice to see my hard work acknowledged.

"Thank you," I tell him. "That means... That means a lot to me," I admit. He glances back at me, his wings rustling again, the iridescence catching the light streaming through the round window that helps the plants in this room grow.

His expression is open in a way I don't think I've seen before. It's almost as if a weight has been lifted from his shoulders, the way he moves around the shop looking at everything with the fresh eyes of someone who's never been inside of it before and can't quite believe what they're seeing.

It's strange, the way it makes me choke up a little. I wonder when the last time it was that I looked at anything with the type of wonder that's so clear in Kieran's face in this moment. When did I last look at the world with childlike appreciation?

The thought makes my heart hurt, and the pain surprises me.

When did the magic of doing magic disappear?

"Do you usually work before eating?" he asks, frowning.

"Are you hungry?" I ask, genuinely curious. "There are some edible plants in the greenhouse if you can't wait."

"Can't wait for what?" he asks. "Do you want me to make you a feast, my sweet green witch?"

My palms fly to my cheeks and, sure enough, they are hot to the touch. I wish that I could tell my body to stop reacting to his out-of-character comments. He doesn't mean them, how could he? He doesn't know who I am. He doesn't even know who he is.

So why is my body acting like this means something?

I don't think I've been this flustered in the better part of a decade, not since I was a young witch.

"There are some berries," I tell him, my voice slightly strangled. "The raspberries are in the final fall flush in the greenhouse. Help yourself."

"You don't want me to make us a feast, green witch?" he asks. Kieran quickly closes the distance between us, a predatory light in his eyes that leaves me near quaking. My boots aren't even laced up. At this rate I'm going to fall out of them before I have a chance to tie them into little bows. He tilts his head, his eyes raking across my body with obvious pleasure.

Everything tightens inside of me and I stare up at him, confused and at a total loss for how to react.

His smile widens, the corners of his eyes crinkling as he grins down at me. "Or, if you prefer," he purrs, "we could make a feast of you, little green witch."

I sputter. I am unequipped to deal with him right now. "Go eat some raspberries," I blurt.

"Hm. I don't think that will have quite the same effect as what I am craving," he says.

My eyes are open so wide in pure shock that it's a wonder they aren't drying out immediately from the effort.

Kieran laughs, a musical, deep sound that resonates within my very bones.

"Are you calling me green witch because you don't remember my name?" I finally ask, leaning on the counter.

"Oh no," he answers, smirking. "I looked through your diary on your nightstand before I joined you out here, I'm well aware that your name is Willow. And I'm well aware that you've been harboring certain thoughts about me for a long time now."

My jaw drops open. "You, you—you didn't."

Amusement dances across the Unseelie prince's face. "No," he drawls. "I didn't read it. All I did was look at the cover for your name. But the fact that you haven't argued with my outlandish comment means I'm not far from the mark, am I?"

I make a noise somewhere between a shrill owl screech and a fox scream. Kieran just laughs some more and swaggers through the greenhouse door, leaving me staring after him in confusion.

CHAPTER 4

KIERAN

I would say that I've never been as attracted to anyone as I am to the luscious, plump-bodied, redhaired which. However, I don't remember being attracted to anyone.

No matter. I know how I feel about her now, and based on the way she blushes every time I look at her, she's lying if she says she doesn't feel the same about me. I grin to myself, completely smug at the newfound knowledge. Knowledge I didn't even have to work hard for, considering the little white lie about reading her journal made it clear exactly what she feels about me.

I frown. But if she feels that way about me, why is she so embarrassed by it? Sweet little Willow, embarrassed by how she feels?

Frustrated at my lack of understanding of the situation, as well as the fact that I am incapable of remembering how I came to be in the situation, I stalk over to the wrought-iron cart labeled "edible plants" and begin to peruse the selection. It turns out losing one's memory does, in fact, make one quite hungry.

I truly am quite impressed with the witch's abilities. The little wheeled cart is chock full of all sorts of plants that, based on the orange and red leaves hanging just outside the greenhouse, aren't even close to in season. In a large pot in the corner a glossy-leaved tree hangs heavy with orange globes. Another small tree boasts a vibrant array of cherries. A small tree next to it has at least 10 different varieties of apples all clinging to the various branches and at different stages of ripening.

The cart itself is full of berries, just as Willow said. I take a few, not wanting to disturb whatever plan she has for them, and slowly savor the first of them against my teeth as I take stock of the wonders of her greenhouse. The middle boasts the largest plant of all—a tree with a thick trunk, scarred from some effort to harvest the bark, I presume. My nostrils flare as I sniff at it, scent familiar and spicy, and lingering with the delicate flavor of the berries on my tongue.

There is a strange flower that seems to pulse with magic. Creamy petals fade into deep purple at the center, and the bloom itself is twice the size of my head. There's no real scent to it save for the scent of pure magic—an unfettered, powerful one at that.

I inhale deeply, studying the plant in confusion. I feel that I should know what it is—that I should recognize the type of magic that's clearly emanating from it, but I don't. It troubles me.

I continue to wander around the greenhouse as I pop berry after berry into my mouth, pausing once to circle back and pluck an apple from a heavy bough. The apple crunches under my teeth, just as flavorful as the berries. A heady, spicy aroma makes its way into my nostrils. It smells incredible.

I reached for the leaves of the plant with the enticing odor, laughing to myself as I read the handwritten sign, "handle with care," which I now recognize as Willow's handwriting.

Carefully I pick up the potted plant, and the leaves give a little shake as if they are saying hello. Which is surely a flight of fancy, yet I find myself staring at them in delight nonetheless.

"What are you?" I ask. I tilt the pot slightly to better read the hand-stamped label on the terra-cotta. "Horny goat weed," I read out loud. It smells edible. Better than edible, really. I might as well try it. Besides, the label only says "handle with care," it doesn't say "not for Unseelie fae ingestion." If I wasn't supposed to eat it, then it shouldn't smell so good.

I pluck off one of the waxy purple-veined leaves and pop it into my mouth, slightly more bitter than the aroma led me to believe but not that much is poisonous to the Unseelie fae race. It's funny how I don't remember exactly who I am or where I came from, but that I know little facts like that about myself.

I chew the leaf thoughtfully, spicy aroma overpowering the bitterness. I swallow and take another leaf and before long, a very pleasant fiery feeling simmers through my veins. It doesn't take long before the plant is stripped nearly entirely.

I hum to myself in confusion. Maybe it has been longer than I realized. No sooner has the thought occurred to me than Willow bursts through the door of the greenhouse, as beautiful as ever.

Her gaze drops to the denuded plant in my hand… then further, to the hand around my cock.

"That's strange," I muse. "How did that get there?"

Her lovely face pinches in annoyance, though I swear I see a hint of a smile at the corners of her lush pink lips.

That's all it takes, just a hint of a smile, and I'm grinning back at her like a lovestruck fool. Of course the image of myself might be slightly undone by the fact that my cock is hard, and in my hand, and I can't seem to stop stroking it.

"Spit. That. Out." Willow enunciates each word carefully, and for some reason, it strikes me as completely hilarious. I burst into laughter, the sound echoing off the glass walls.

It's strange that my own laughter sounds so foreign to my ears. The thought sobers me somewhat, although I can't seem to stop stroking my cock.

I'm starting to think I should be concerned about that fact; unfortunately I can't find myself to be concerned about much of anything except for the fact that my cock desperately wants someone else stroking it.

I raise an eyebrow, the corner of my lip starting up into a half smile.

To my shock, her hand flies up and she slaps the remaining few leaves out of my fingers. "This is exactly why you shouldn't be eating things when you don't know what they are," she hisses.

I stare at her for a long moment, bewildered by her sudden anger. "Is it poisonous? Worse?"

She looses an exasperated sigh that's so forceful I'm surprised it doesn't knock her down.

"No, but that doesn't mean you should just be eating the entire plant."

I grip my cock, stroking it frenetically, realizing that it's beginning to get a bit uncomfortable. Her eyebrows shoot up and she glances down at my package meaningfully.

"This is exactly what I'm talking about," she says.

"There's nothing wrong with it," I say. "It's natural to be aroused in the presence of a beautiful female such as yourself."

"It's not natural if it's caused by eating an entire plant of horny goat weed," she screeches.

"But—"

"No butts about it herein." She glares at me. "You're going to have a boner for the rest of the day, and you know what? It's not my problem." She throws up her hands, her lip curled in disgust. "It's your fault you ate an entire horny goat weed and that you're going to have blue balls that ache for likely the rest of the month."

I shrug one shoulder, still stroking myself. "It's not really a problem if I can find someone to help relieve that ache." I wink at her outrageously. "So you're saying you're not volunteering for the job?"

She glares at me but her cheeks pinken once more. I truly enjoy the effect my words have on her.

"Get your hands out of your pants," she utters, her eyes darkening, but with anger, not with the sultry passion I would prefer. "We have to figure out what we're going to do with you. Hopefully a strong cup of tea and maybe a charmed piece of pastry will take the edge off of what you just did to yourself."

"Oh," I purr, bending closer and catching the delicious scent of her skin. "Did you want me to call you my little pastry now, Willow?"

My little green witch looses what could be considered a ferocious roar from a newborn kitten. I laugh again, utterly delighted.

She points a finger at me, prodding it into my chest. I groan, because that's all it takes for a bead of precum to begin dripping from the tip of my cock.

"Hands. Out. Of. Your. Pants." She mumbles something under her breath, and I get the feeling I'm not supposed to hear it, but she must've forgotten that I have superior hearing. "Need a lot more than one pastry to deal with this nonsense," she grumbles.

"Why, my little pastry, my sweet little chocolate croissant, you could deal with my nonsense all by yourself if only you wanted to."

With a look of pure derision, she flounces out of the greenhouse, leaving me to follow in her wake, my laughter echoing off the glass walls.

CHAPTER 5

WILLOW

By the time we make it to The Pixie's Perch, some of my ire has worn off, replaced by a childish fascination with the fact that Kieran is completely overwhelmed physically by the horny goat weed's effects. From a purely scientific standpoint, seeing the reaction on the full-blooded male fae prince is enlightening.

From the completely petty standpoint of the woman whose life he's made miserable for the past few weeks, I take a sick sort of pleasure from his obvious discomfort. I don't like it about myself that his discomfort is amusing to me, but he brought it on himself.

So here we are.

I veritably tow him behind me into town, bypassing the long willow-bough broom by The Pixie's Perch that I normally nod to in greeting in favor of getting something into the poor prince as soon as possible. Kieran, for his part, is making a sort of low tortured noise, and despite my petty amusement, I am starting to get a bit worried about the effects of the aforementioned horny goat weed.

The town center is packed with people.

I pause in my crusade to get to the bottom of whatever is going on with Kieran as soon as possible, in pure shock. The tents that we set up for the autumn festival are still raised in the center of town. And in fact, the entire town center teams with the citizens of Wild Oak Woods.

A group of rowdy dwarves are cutting up in the corner closest to the pastry displays at the tent entrance. They are about the only group I notice before pulling Kieran through the crowd. A minotaur I wedge in front of lets out a distinctly moo-sounding exclamation of disgruntlement that prompts Kieran to turn over one shoulder and level him with the nastiest look possible on his pretty face.

The minotaur takes a step back.

Can't say I blame him.

I clear my throat, waiting for Piper to finish handing a pretty pink ribbon-tied box full of pastries to Lila, the proprietor of the town's tea shop, and notice us.

Piper's long brown hair is tied neatly back into two braids that crisscross and wrap overhead like a crown, her cheeks flushed from the heat of the bakery despite the chill of the fall air outside. Ga'Rek is at her side, and his pleasant, welcoming expression turns to one of confusion as Kieran stares at him as though he's never seen him before in his life.

It must be clear from the expression on my face that something is very, very wrong, because Piper immediately takes me by the arm and pulls me behind the table still laden with the feast from last night. The scent of magic is in the air, and it's clear that the rest of the witches performed some sort of spell work to keep this table fresh for today's festivities.

Part of me realizes that I should congratulate Piper on being able to pull off the autumn festival despite the terrible circumstances of last night, but I'm starting to get too freaked out about Kieran to do anything but blurt the entirety of our problems to her.

Immediately.

"He's lost his memory," I wail. "He doesn't remember who I am, where we are, or most anything about his past other than his name and the fact that he's an Unseelie fae. I don't know what happened. I didn't cast any spells, I swear it. Even though you know I've been pining after him, there is no way that I would have done anything to warrant this sort of personality change."

"Well, well, well. The truth comes out." Kieran leans against the table, raking his gaze up and down my body.

My entire body cringes, and I cover my face with trembling hands.

Wonderful. This is just what I needed, for Kieran to hear my unfettered thoughts about him. It was one thing when he underhandedly tried to trick me into admitting I have feelings for him, but admitting it here, out in the open, in front of everyone, is a whole different problem.

How do I always find myself in these situations?

"I don't want to hear about it from you," I snap.

"It seems cruel of you not to help me with my current predicament, considering you have the feelings required to make good on exactly what I need help with," Kieran says smugly.

"What?" Ga'Rek scratches his chin in confusion.

He looks exactly how I feel on the inside.

"He lost his memory." Piper glances between the two of us, then looks to Ga'Rek for help.

I shouldn't have put this on her shoulders. It's just one more mess for her to clean up, and she doesn't need that. It's clear my friend could very much use a morning off from the drama of Wild Oak Woods.

Yet here I am, ruining everyone's day, because I can't figure out anything other than how to grow plants.

"I shouldn't bother you with this," I blurt. "I'm so sorry, we'll just go back—"

"We're not going back anywhere until my problem is taken care of," Kieran says, his voice dripping with acid.

"A problem that you caused after eating all of the horny goat weed in the greenhouse." I will not stomp my foot. I will *not*.

"You told me I could help myself to the greenhouse," he sniffs.

"To the fruit," I snarl.

I give myself one foot stomp, because I deserve it.

Ga'Rek and Piper are staring at us with twin expressions of dismay.

"I woke up with him naked in my bed," I say by way of explanation.

Although, judging from the shock that's now simmering across their expressions, I get the feeling I've only made things worse. Again.

"Right," Piper slowly stretches the word out, infusing it with a world of meaning. It makes me feel even smaller than usual.

A heavy hand lands on my shoulder, and I glance up in surprise and gratification as Kieran pulls me close into his body.

"Don't upset her," he growls. "That's no way to talk to her."

The hum of noise turns down, even the merry-makers at the festival falling silent at the pure venom in Kieran's tone.

Piper and Ga'Rek share another look and I try to breathe normally. They seem to be communicating silently, which I'm not sure is even possible.

They're all so much better at magic than I am, it wouldn't surprise me at all to find they could do so.

Ga'Rek raises an eyebrow, staring pointedly at Kieran.

"I see," he says simply.

"Do you think it has something to do with last night?" I ask quietly, so as not to garner more interest from all the listening ears in the tent. "Did the Elder Gods or whatever they call themselves... Do you think that they took his memories away?"

"Absolutely not," Nerissa pipes up.

I hadn't realized she was standing there, listening to everything.

I hold back a sigh. Of course she was.

Her wolf familiar moves silently through the crowd to her side.

He sits on his haunches, pink tongue rolling out of his mouth as he stares up at us. I get the distinct impression that the wolf finds all of this completely hilarious. My own familiar, who, like always, followed me out, lets out a hoot from his perch on one of the star lanterns hung from the silk tent ceiling.

Simply seeing Chirp there makes me feel slightly better and I stand up straight, turning to face Nerissa. Kieran's hand's still heavy on my shoulder. Possessive. "Why do you say that?"

"You don't smell like their magic. You smell like her magic." Nerissa dips her chin at me. "Like green magic. Not the eldritch magic of the Elder Forest or the elementals that apparently have been living within it." She shrugs as though this should be resoundingly obvious to all of us.

Kieran's hand tightens on my shoulder.

"Yes, the unbearably horny residents of the Elder Forest." Caelan, the trickster fae, appears practically out of nowhere, his voice dripping with glee. "As horny as ye old goat of an Unseelie prince, it seems, though not nearly as forgetful."

Piper and I both glare balefully at Caelan, who simply grins and shrugs. "It does smell like your magic, Willow witch."

"Don't presume you have my leave to speak to her in that tone," Kieran snarls, and I blink in shock.

"Your leave?" I repeat, unsure if I'm annoyed Kieran wants to give permission for someone to talk to me or gratified to be stuck up for.

Somewhere in between, probably. I rub my temple.

Caelan, for his part, simply looks smug. Smug, and all too

invested in Kieran's newfound self-designated role as my protector.

"So, you're finally ready to admit it to us all how you feel about Willow," Caelan drawls, pressing his fingertips against the top of the long table. A large cake teeters precariously on the stand next to him.

He must be exerting quite a bit of pressure to make it do that. Which means he must not be as calm, cool, and collected as he prides himself on being.

"Kieran doesn't know what he feels about me," I say. "He can't even remember any of you, much less form an opinion about me."

"I'm standing right here," Kieran says, iciness creeping into his voice. "I will be the judge of how I feel about you, my little croissant."

Nerissa bites her lips as if to keep from laughing, and even Ears makes a loud whuffing noise as if in disbelief.

Heat shoots up from my chest to my throat to my face, and I know I've turned as red as my hair.

"I am not your croissant," I say. The effectiveness of the declaration is somewhat hampered by the fact that I sound pathetically wispy when uttering it.

I try again.

"I am not your croissant?"

Great, now it just sounds like I'm asking a question.

He stares down his nose at me, a muscle in his temple twitching. "If I want you to be my little croissant, you will be my little croissant."

The heat flooding my body has less to do now with embarrassment than it does with a heightened awareness of how close all of that muscled purple skin is to me.

I'm in danger.

I already had a massive... thing for Kieran.

I had no idea how dangerous it could be if he returned the feeling, even just a little bit.

"I'm not your croissant." I repeat.

"Soft, delicious, and ready to be eaten or filled. Croissant fits you perfectly."

I grind my molars, squeezing my eyes shut and counting backwards.

"There are definitely worse pastries to be called," Caelan says, and Nerissa snorts.

Caelan claps his hands together in delight. "Can we call her your croissant, too?"

Without the pressure of his hands, the tall layer cake stops quivering. Piper breathes a sigh of relief.

For his part, Ga'Rek shoots Caelan a quelling look, which accomplishes absolutely nothing. Caelan, I assume, has never been one to be quelled.

Wren finally joins us, placing an arm on Caelan's wrist, and he gives her a worshipful look that takes his focus off us.

"You're mated." Kieran's words come out on a shocked exhalation.

I glance up at the prince, and his eyes are wide.

"How? I didn't think the fae could form a mate bond with any species other than our own."

"How do you even remember that?" I ask, throwing up my hands. Goddess, this is the worst. Is he trying to form a mate bond with me?

I blow out a harsh breath and try to rein in my emotions.

It's either that or just start screaming and never stop.

Wren elbows Caelan sharply in the ribs before he can form a reply, but he doesn't seem to care, simply grinning at her pointedly before turning back to Kieran.

"You seem very interested in mating someone who isn't fae," he says casually. His eyes glitter, belying his latent amusement.

Wren elbows him again, harder this time.

I make a mental note to buy some more jewelry from her. And maybe ask to be tutored on how to control a wayward fae.

"Are you considering a permanent bond to your croissant? Perhaps splitting her open and buttering her?"

Outrage fills me.

Wren utters his name in a deadly tone, and this time, he winces.

It's too late, though.

Now I'm mad.

"I have had enough," I sputter. "Your friend, the friend that you followed from the Underhill to Wild Oak Woods, has amnesia. Amnesia. Memory loss. And it's caused by some magic that I don't understand, and all you can do is make terrible jokes at his expense about me? It wasn't even a good joke. Your material needs work."

Caelan opens his mouth to respond, looking wounded at my criticism more than my reprimand, but I raise a hand and cut him off before he has the chance to say anything.

My hand stops just short of making contact with his face.

Truly, I should win a prize for my inhuman restraint.

"You should be ashamed of yourself; he is supposed to be your friend. Something terrible has happened, and all you can do is whatever sad excuse for humor this is?"

"My humor is honed in dark fae magic—"

"SAVE YOUR PASTRY JOKES FOR SOMEONE ELSE," I bellow.

Kieran's fingers tighten on my shoulder.

Slowly, they run down over the fabric of my sleeve to rest on my elbow, and he presses me tighter against him.

My chest heaves from the indignity of it all. And the fact that I'm slightly out of breath from screaming.

Well, everyone in the tent is certainly staring now.

Nerissa's watching the whole affair unfold with interest, picking profiteroles off a platter and popping them in her mouth at regular intervals.

"I can be two things at once," Caelan tells me.

There's an air of insouciant superiority about him, and it reminds me of all the stories my mother and her coven told me about the fae when I was but a young girl.

That the fae are mercurial, that they are not to be trusted, and above all that they care nothing for us humans, witches or not.

I turn my attention to Wren, curious how she can stand to be around the trickster at all, much less romantically involved with him. Forever. While she seems slightly exasperated with Caelan, Wren doesn't seem overly offended by his antics.

On the contrary, she's glancing between Kieran and me as though she's seeing us both for the first time.

Wren's expression, however, tells me that she had no idea that I felt so strongly for Kieran. She even manages to throw a hurt look my way.

Like I should have told her about how I felt for him.

The realization confuses me.

I thought that I'd at least mentioned it to them in passing, but apparently they're as surprised by this turn of events as Kieran himself.

I need to get this conversation back on track.

This is not the time to be wondering about why my friends can't read my mind and why I would assume that they could in the first place. No, it's high time to figure out how to restore Kieran's memories and get to the bottom of why it happened in the first place.

"This doesn't have anything to do with the Elder Forest elementals, if that's what you're trying to get out," says Nerissa seriously.

Her usual flair for dramatic proclamations has been abandoned in the face of our predicament.

Thank the goddess.

"They want brides. They want to fulfill some ancient contract our coven made for our protection. The seriousness of the Elder Gods requesting brides from us, as bad as that is, has nothing to do with..." She trails off, waving her hand at Kieran vaguely, "this."

"What is all this talk about Elder Gods?" Kieran says with pronounced derision. "No Elder God or elemental would dare take a witch away from me."

The matter-of-fact pronouncement halts my thoughts entirely.

"I don't know what you think I am to you, or what you think you are to me... but I do not belong to you." I'm perturbed.

Extremely perturbed.

Not so much by his words... but by how much I like them. I sigh deeply, then pinch the bridge of my nose.

How completely messed up is that?

Pretty damned messed up.

"I don't know what we are to each other at all," Kieran tells me quietly. He leans down so the softness of his lips brushes against the top of my ear.

If I weren't already beet-red, I would for sure be now.

"But I do know that I would like us to be something in the future. Do with that what you must, my delectable little croissant, but I think we both know deep down that you're amenable to the possibility."

I find myself sorely wishing that I hadn't laced my overdress on so tightly this morning. It's a bit hard to breathe. Harder every time he says something like that, in fact.

Then again, from the way Kieran eyes the swell of my breasts, I don't think he has any complaints with the way I laced my dress.

"I'm sorry to say, Willow, I agree with Nerissa. I don't think whatever's going on with Kieran has anything to do with what happened last night." Piper wrings her hands together.

"I'm also sorry to say that the demand of three forest gods—beings we didn't even know existed before last night—rank higher on our immediate priority list than restoring Kieran's memory. He is safe with you, isn't he?" Nerissa asks, tilting her head.

"Of course he is safe with me," I sputter, offended all over again.

That's me, just a blushing ball of offended sensibilities and weak plant magic who doesn't rank high enough on the coven priority list to garner more support than whatever it is I'm getting now.

"What Nerissa is trying to say," Piper starts softly, "is that Kieran should probably stay with you. Whatever happened to him has something to do with your magic, and you'll most likely figure it out if you simply retrace your steps and work together."

It's a mark of how sad and lonely I've been that I can't even think of one reason to tell them that is a very terrible idea.

It's a mark of how obsessed I've been with Kieran that I don't immediately tell them that it's a terrible idea. It's a mark of how terrible a person I am that I think it might actually be a very good idea.

For very selfish reasons that have nothing to do with solving the amnesia mystery.

"I'm sorry to interrupt," a soft voice I don't immediately recognize chimes in.

The group of us turns, and the newest witch to town stands before us, arms crossed over her body.

There's something incredibly delicate about her fine bone structure, especially paired with her overly large eyes. The latter practically swallow up her face, stark brown and undeniably sad.

"No one explained to me why it is they appeared last night. Those three beings, I mean." Her cheeks suck in, as if she's biting them. Paired with the look of deep regret on her face for calling our attention to her, my heart immediately goes out to her.

I fight the urge to give Violet a long hug and tell her everything's going to be all right. She just looks like she could use someone to take care of her.

"Lucky for you all, I was up most of the night scouring through my shelves." Ruby Walks, owner of the town's Listening Page Bookstore, does, in fact, look like she spent the entire night wide awake. Dark circles hang heavy beneath her eyes. Her skin's lost its healthy luster for a slightly more sallow shade.

Goddess, I have been so selfish.

I ran from the coven's problems last night to nurse my own sense of woundedness, then threw Kieran's new issues at them instead of considering how what happened last night is affecting everyone else.

I wince when she glances at me.

Ruby scoffs, and I ready myself for a well-deserved verbal flagellation.

"Don't you dare look at me like that," Ruby says.

Here we go.

"I stayed up late because I wanted to; the last thing I need is to be joined at the hip to some overly powerful being that we just learned the existence of to save our town from some existential threat we didn't even know existed."

I blink.

Ruby clears her throat, looking around a little wildly. Her familiar winds in between her legs, his fluffy tail held like a plume behind him as he lets out a plaintive yowl.

Ruby bends to pick him up. His tufted ears flatten on the back of his head as he surveys us all like a king might his court.

She coughs delicately, looking chagrined. "No one was thinking that, were they?"

"Has everyone forgotten of my condition? And I'm not talking about the amnesia, or whatever you want to call this." Kieran points to his head, his voice strained. "I'm talking about the boner that will not go away." His points to his other head.

I can't help it. I burst into laughter.

I clap a hand over my mouth, horrified at how horrible it is to laugh at this. Everyone seems caught between shock and awe at both Kieran's pronouncement and my very ill-timed giggle fit.

As for Kieran, though, he looks down at me with a soft smile. More than anything, that's what finally makes my laughter stop.

"I might be able to help with the Elder Gods," a deep voice rings out. Druze, a male dryad of staggering size, is looking on from outside our little circle. "I can tell you what I know."

Lila, his wife, stands with her arms folded gently around a thick towel. It steams lightly, the cloud rising around the pointed tips of the elfin ears poking out through her light blonde hair.

"He can help with that," Lila agrees with a smile. "And I brought some tea. I had an inkling that, ah, someone might be a bit too excitable this morning."

Kieran turns to her immediately and tugs the covered pot from her hands. The towel falls away to reveal a teapot the shape and color of a winter cabbage. More steam pours from the spout.

"Careful, it's very hot," Lila advises, wincing as Kieran manhandles the delicate vessel.

"How did you know what he needed?" Ga'Rek asks. He winds his massive arm around Piper's waist, holding her protectively against him.

It must be nice to be held like that by someone who knows who you are.

Without Kieran's arm around me, occupied as he is with the tea, I feel oddly cold.

"Chirp might have tattled on you to Rosalina," Lila says to Kieran. "That owl is very worried about what you might do to Willow in your, ah, delicate condition." She arches an eyebrow at me, and I hide my smile.

My heart swells momentarily for my familiar, who did exactly what needed to be done to help Kieran, and by extension, me. I don't know what I did to deserve a familiar like Chirp in my life, but I'm grateful he's in it.

I might be lonely, but I'm not alone.

Druze helps himself to a slice of cake dressed carefully in sugared swirls, peppered with strawberries sourced from my greenhouse. A little jolt of pride goes through me at the sight of the red berries against white cake.

I hold my head a little higher. I might not be as magical or talented as the other witches, but I am good at what I do.

"Tell us what you know, man," Ga'Rek all but growls, clearly sick of waiting for his information.

Druze chews thoughtfully before slowly swallowing.

"The dryads speak of gods in the forest."

We're all hanging on his every syllable already.

"We had myths and legends about them," he continues.

"Is there anyone in your community that might know more about them?" Ruby urges, twitching slightly, clearly ready for him to speed it up.

I don't blame her.

"I always just thought that they were myths and legends," Druze says shrugging his shoulders. "Others might know more than I do, but I wouldn't be sure of it."

He pauses.

Can't get a tree to hurry for anything, I guess.

"Besides, dryads don't like to talk to outsiders much."

Ruby sighs, and Ga'Rek moves closer to Druze.

"Tell us what you do know, then," he says. "Everything. Nothing's too small."

"Why are *you* so worried about this?" Caelan interrupts, his forehead wrinkled in confusion. "You have a mate, so she's not in danger of being taken."

Ga'Rek fixes him with an irritated look. Despite the orc's good nature, it's easy to see how quickly he could shift to dangerous.

For his part, Druze doesn't quell under Ga'Rek's fierce gaze.

Instead, he simply inclines his head and then begins to speak again.

"I was raised with the stories. Always told in hushed tones when the nights grew longer and darker, so dark and it seemed that the sun would never rise again. The stories were passed down by the eldest of the dryads. They had thicker trunks than you can imagine, and barrel chests, and a note of truth in their voices."

He pauses, and from the way Ruby's shifting from foot to foot, I can tell she's a heartbeat away from yelling at him to get on with it.

"No one ever spoke of them too loudly, or around too many people. We all heard stories of the forest elementals, these Elder Gods, nonetheless. They took the blame for anything ill that arose, and yet were thanked for anything good happening."

He exhales slowly, and Lila nudges him gently with her elbow.

Good, because I might help Ruby shake the words loose if he doesn't hurry it up.

"Not in any way that was overt, or even truly ritualized, but with small trinkets left at the edge of the forest, or honey and fruit left in the same places. They would be gone by morning." He shrugs one shoulder, and his placid expression turns troubled. "When I was a child, I was enchanted by the idea of actual elder beings wandering the depths of the forest. Elementals, pure magic made physical. Incredible." He shakes his head, still apparently taken with the idea.

Ruby lets out a soft huff of annoyance, her lips thin in impatience.

"As I grew older, I realized animals most likely took the food. The trinkets could have been squirreled away by racoons or magpies. The stories of the Elder Gods were dismissed amongst my peers and me as an elder's way to coerce the younger generation to behave. Still, our elders' habits and fear of speaking of them too loudly stayed with us." His expression turns thoughtful. "This is likely the first time I've discussed them in decades."

Caelan sighs. "Is that all? I'm not sure how helpful any of that drivel was."

What an asshole. I'm not sure how Wren can stand him.

"Then you should probably let me finish," Druze says. He cracks his knuckles, and Caelan sniffs.

Next to him, Lila sighs wearily and then gives me a pointed look.

As for Kieran, he's foregone the cups Lila brought. Nope, no cups for him. He's drinking the piping hot tea straight from the top of the adorable cabbage-shaped pot.

Right. Of course he is.

"The main theme of the stories passed down amongst my people about the three Elder Gods was that they were protectors of the forest and even the towns and people that lived on the outskirts of it." He gestures broadly around with a green hand, clearly trying to signify Wild Oak Woods. "But they were not protectors without a price. Every so often, they would manifest and demand something from those whom they protected, whether or not they ever invoked them and asked for their protection. Was only ever in great times of need, like in the redwood wars several centuries ago or in the deep winter fires more recently." He shakes his head. "You can understand why we would think them to be fiction. Maybe it was wishful thinking, because the thought of such a vast power and the price it may exact is frightening. But there's also a certain comfort in the idea that something you cannot fully understand is trying to help you in ways that you may never see." He shrugs again, and his eyebrows lift in time with his shoulders.

"Now we know what they want," Nerissa says, crossing her arms over her chest. "They want us."

Druze nods his head in agreement. "They want you. And I've never heard of them asking for anything like that. Food, yes. Tokens of gratitude, yes. Livestock? Yes. But never a bride."

"I think it's worth asking the question of why the prices are going up for their protection," Ruby says slowly.

A shiver goes down my spine as what she's suggesting finally materializes in my mind.

"What is so terrifying that they require the payment of three brides as the price to protect Wild Oak Woods?"

I find myself looking at Druze, trying to deduce if he has the answers to any of the questions racing through my mind.

Violet shifts, chewing her lower lip nervously, her eyes darting around before finally settling on Piper. "But if we could ask them, should we?"

"What do you—" Caelan starts, but Wren holds a hand up to stop him from speaking.

"Are they here right now?" Piper's voice is hushed, and the hair on the back of my neck stands up.

Kieran abandons the teapot on the table and narrows his eyes at me.

Before I can clock what he's about to do, he wraps his arms around me, pulling me tight to his chest.

I choke out a little cough, sure my eyes are near bugging out of my head, because—

"Can't breathe," I wheeze.

His grip loosens slightly. Which is to say, not very much at all. I gulp down the little air he allows.

Violet's eyes are wide as saucers, her gaze darting between where Kieran's arm is around me like a vise, and what I assume to be his expression behind me.

A quick look up verifies my suspicions.

Yep.

His lips are pulled back in a snarl; the gorgeous iridescent wings I've spent too many hours avoiding staring at are on full display behind him.

Oh. Oh my.

His eyes, normally a deeper purplish blue, are nearly full black, something I've never seen before.

"Easy boy," I choke out.

"Not really," Violet finally answers slowly, dragging the words out and looking beyond Kieran.

Beyond the crowded tent and the citizens of Wild Oak Woods milling about.

Caelan clears his throat meaningfully, and Ga'Rek looms larger than ever.

If there was a looming contest, the orc warrior would win it, hands down.

"Then where are they?" Ga'Rek growls. His eyes glitter. None of the good humor I've begun to associate with the orc remains.

Violet quails under his menacing perusal.

"They sent a spirit guide," she says, her voice uncertain. "It said they just wanted to talk. They don't understand why we're upset."

Piper puts a delicate hand on Ga'Rek's wrist and he audibly swallows, nodding nearly imperceptibly.

"Forgive me, Violet," he says in his deep voice.

"Continue," Piper tells her.

I stare openly at the pair of them with pure admiration. Amazing how quickly they've become in tune with each other. I've always admired Piper's quiet way of leading, her way of knowing exactly how to anticipate what people want and need and then help them get it.

The two of them are a force already.

"I don't understand what else it's saying exactly." Violet wrings her hands. "I don't know what else they're trying to tell us. I'm sorry. I wish I did."

I don't know what's happened to this fragile new witch, but from the way she seems afraid of everything, I can only imagine what she's been through on her way to us.

"Do your best to explain," Nerissa tells her, not unkindly. The black-haired witch, our spell maker, steps forward and braces her hands on Violet's elbows. "We all had to start from somewhere," Nerissa tells her. "We understand this is new to you. We all know new things can be just as scary as they are exciting, sometimes even more so."

I tried to bring myself to remember what it was like to live a life without magic before my powers fully set the summer I turned thirteen. I can't.

There was never a time in my life when I didn't have magic, when I didn't find all plants to be full of magic.

"It says what happens now happened before... I guess a long time ago. It doesn't understand time like we do... and that the elementals manifested then, here, just like they are now...but they've never demanded a bride tribute."

Her words tumble over themselves, her eyes far away, as if she's translating something that's being said to her and trying to keep up as best she can.

"The spirit says the balance has never been so..." She shakes her head. "I don't understand what it's saying, something about a wheel spinning out of control, or maybe a scale?"

She looks to Nerissa for help. Even Nerissa can't speak to spirits.

Nerissa squeezes her elbows encouragingly and Violet closes her eyes.

"There's a balance of magic, of power, dark and light, I think," Violet says slowly. Magic shifts around us, nothing like the kind I wield, and it tickles over my skin. "There is a wild magic in the Elder Forest, or beyond it? I don't know. A wild magic that's been caged? Or contained? By previous covens. The elementals can balance the chaos, but they need the help of a bound witch... or three."

"A counterweight." Nerissa runs a hand through her hair. "That... makes sense."

I have no idea what she means by that. From the consternated expression on Wren's face, I get the feeling she has no idea, either.

Great. A coven full of plant and kitchen and jewelry witches up against pure chaos power.

And Nerissa, whose spell making capabilities are great, sure, but she's more prone to drama than exerting true power.

A flurry of voices eclipses Nerissa's mutterings.

We've drawn a crowd around us. Magic hangs heavy in the air around Violet and Nerissa.

The new witch's eyes are wide, unseeing. An invisible force whips her hair around her head.

It's like nothing I've ever seen before.

Fear worms inside my heart, and we have much bigger problems than Kieran's lost memories.

Like he senses I'm thinking of him, Kieran's breath warms the shell of my ear. Goosebumps rise along my skin that have nothing to do with the threat to our way of life and everything to do with his body nestled into mine.

"There," Nerissa tells Violet, patting her arms. "You did well, you did so well."

Ruby looks frankly at Nerissa. "I've seen no mention of any of this in the town records, nor the coven records."

It's Violet that answers. "Wild magic was expunged from the histories."

Ruby's expression turns to outrage. "Expunged from the histories," she repeats. "That is against the historians' code of honor." She places a hand over her heart and Caelan lets out a low chuckle at the witch's ire.

"There's a name for that in the Underhill," he says with a grin that doesn't quite meet his eyes. "We call it the queen's version."

The look of disdain Ruby spears him with is the harshest I've ever seen from the witch. I would not like to be on the receiving end of it.

Although, judging from Kieran's glower, I'm not much at risk for even a mean look at the moment. It shouldn't feel as nice as it does.

"Wild magic," Nerissa muses, tapping the end of her nose with her forefinger. The light of the multicolored lanterns overhead reflects warmly in the gloss of her black hair.

"It's all rather exciting," she says rubbing her hands together with gusto.

"For you, maybe," I say, exasperated. "Some of us aren't strong spell casters. Some of us aren't good at anything but growing plants. Some of us don't want to get married to some ancient elemental power because we can't do anything else to help."

Oh goddess.

I've shouted it at her.

Goddess dammit.

"I didn't mean it like that," I say, my voice faltering. "I just don't know how I can help protect our home. It's not exciting to me. It's terrifying."

Wren winces sympathetically at me.

The angry sound of Kieran's wings intensifies behind me. "Of course you can protect your home," he says, and the anger in his voice startles me, startles everyone as a thousand eyes gaze up at the Unseelie prince. "I don't know who's convinced you that your power doesn't matter as much as these other witches', but they were sorely mistaken. None of them would be able to do their best work without you."

"He's absolutely right," says Nerissa, nodding her head. I scour her face for a hint of sarcasm, but find none. "You are an integral part of our coven, and of the whole community writ large." Nerissa raises her eyebrows at me and smiles as a chorus of agreement sounds from all around me.

Not just from my coven, but from all the citizens of Wild Oak Woods who stopped merry-making to listen to our heated conversation.

"You saved my crop of apple trees this fall."

"You brewed the potion that kept my babies' fevers at bay," another voice calls.

"Willow's greenhouse is full of the plants that allow me to make everything I sell," Piper adds gently, smiling at me.

A rousing cheer goes up around us, and my cheeks heat. Kieran's arm loosens slightly around my waist, his thumb brushing a stroke across the soft flesh of my stomach in a way that sends my blood hot and singing through me.

"We don't need them," a voice bellows, running through the noise of the crowd. One of the minotaur builders shakes a fist at Violet as though she's the reason the Elder Gods are here, instead of simply the messenger.

She draws inward, and it breaks my heart to see her retreat further into the shell of herself.

"That's right, we don't need their damned help!" his brother yells out, stamping his hooves. His cheeks are bright red, the honey mead in his hand sloshing over the stein's rim.

"Don't you dare blame Violet," Nerissa says, and energy crackles off of her skin. "She delivered the message. She didn't compose it. What exactly do you propose to do differently?"

The minotaur brothers have the courtesy to look rightfully abashed in the wake of her words.

"What we are *not* going to do is make decisions in anger and fear when they affect all of us—not just our coven," Piper declares in that kind, no-nonsense way of hers that I so admire. Murmurs of agreement trickle through the crowd.

Agreement, fervent in their belief that Piper does know best. They're confident that she's offered is the best solution.

"You need protection," Darius, the older of the minotaur brothers, says, and the younger brother chimes in immediately, "Each of the witches needs protection." His eyes dart to me and Kieran's wings beat an angry frenzy behind us both so hard that it pushes the hair against my face.

Undeterred by the angry Unseelie behind me, the younger

minotaur, Donovan, continues, "I wouldn't mind guarding Willow."

"Willow's mine," Kieran snarls.

My eyebrows rocket up in surprise. It's one thing to surmise someone's grown possessive of you and it's quite another to hear it enunciated loud enough for the entire town, the words of warning warm against your skin. I swallow hard trying to think my way through my current predicament. On the one hand, it's as though my wishes have been heard, and on the other, I'm afraid to learn at what cost. This isn't the Kieran I know. The Kieran I know wouldn't care if I offered myself up to dear Donovan and Darius, brothers of the bovine persuasion. I cough delicately, which Kieran seems to take as consent to being called his because the next thing I know, we're airborne.

Kieran's beautiful green wings graze the top of the tent, one of the multicolored lamps teetering dangerously as he flies by. He clutches me tight against him, his wings buzzing furiously.

Words fail me.

I force my gaze back down. My coven stares up at me with expressions ranging from aghast to amused.

The ground is really, really far away, and I squeeze my eyes shut.

Looking down was a mistake.

"Make sure to protect her," Nerissa calls merrily.

I can hear laughing, and another stupid look down shows Caelan doubled over in laughter.

If they hadn't all been so sure that the magic smelled like mine, I would bet money that the trickster was behind this change in Kieran's heart... well, his entire lack of memory, that is.

If the circumstances were different, there's no doubt in my mind that I would be thrilled with my current situation.

It's just my luck that he doesn't have a clue who I am, nor does he remember whatever grudge he held against me.

Terrible luck, that is.

CHAPTER 6

KIERAN

I hate that I can feel the terror traveling through Willow's perfectly plump curves as I fly with her in my arms. It's a short trip back to her quaint stone cottage and lovely glass greenhouse, but feels all too long to get away from the prying eyes of the villagers and the magic of her sister witches.

"You're safe," I tell her, brushing my lips against her ear.

She trembles again, and I wonder how she's so afraid of what I love most in the world: flying. At least, I think it is.

I purse my lips, trying to conjure a memory of it before now.

Nothing's there.

Self-doubt tickles the back of my mind, but it melts away when I realize that Willow is not trembling in fear at all—no, she's trembling with barely-contained laughter.

"What's so funny?" I demand, wanting to be in on the joke.

I need to know what it is that's made her create the most beautiful sound I've ever heard.

She doesn't answer the question, though, instead responding

with even more laughter, leaving me to guess at the source of her merriment.

The weathered wood shingles of Willow's roof quickly draw into view. An icy breeze whips from the edges of the thick forest, the boundary of the Wild Oak Woods visible here where she lives at the very perimeter of town

I set down gently, my wings strangely tired from the effort of flying. Is flying, despite the pure joy of it, something I typically don't do? I frown, struggling to remember why I wouldn't fly when it seems as natural as breathing.

And then Willow turns to face me fully, the pure joy on her lovely face banishing all thoughts other than her.

I want to wrap my arms around her, soak in the heat of her deliciously curved and soft body.

"That was unexpected," she says, her lips twisted into a smirk, an expression I'd very much like to freeze on her face forever.

This smile is much preferable to the annoyance and sadness that's hung heavy over her since waking.

Before I can stop myself, I reach out and touch the corner of her mouth, wanting to memorize the lines of it. I may not have old memories, but this? Willow grinning up at me, happiness shining through her skin? This is something I do not want to forget.

Willow steps back, away from my touch, her smile faltering before melting off her face completely.

Dismay rocks me, and my hand hangs between us before I manage to retract it.

It's the furthest she's been from me since we first arrived in the tent, and I find myself missing the warmth of her body immediately. Immeasurably.

Still, I resist the urge to pull her against me. She doesn't want to be close to me, or she would be. I told her she was mine, I tried to show her how much she should want to be with me, and still, she's afraid… as if she's been ill-treated in the past.

I'll kill whoever dared put that fear in her heart.

Her gaze turns cautious, her pretty green eyes narrowed. Bright red cheeks under her eyes, a token of the cold air whipping around us.

Her glorious fire-red hair is wild, curls unruly and spirited, much the same as Willow the witch herself.

"What's wrong?" The question lingers between us, a sign of how unable I am to help myself when it comes to her.

I know I shouldn't push, so when she takes a moment to consider her answer, I stay silent.

"What was that all about?" she asks. Her hands fly to her hips as though the sharp crack of her elbow will stave me off, as if anything could. I take a step closer, trying her— and she doesn't move away.

Victory emboldens me, and I take a deep breath, trying to steady myself.

And only succeeding in inhaling her intoxicating scent.

"They said we need to keep you safe. I decided that your town square was no longer safe," I say slowly, because isn't it obvious?

Can't she see how real the danger is for her? How close she could come to being ripped from her home and my arms, where she belongs?

Mine.

She stamps her foot, another curl escaping the crown of braids on her head. My wings snap shut behind me, my instinct crying out to conserve energy in case I must pursue this female. In case she runs.

Heat rolls through me at the idea, appealing to me more than it would be honorable to admit.

"Why are you looking at me like that?" She shifts her weight from foot to foot and my instinct insists she contemplates running; a doe chased by a monster.

"I wouldn't go any further," I rasp out.

She freezes, her eyes wide. I lunge towards her before I have time to think it through, only knowing that all my senses are saying I need to grab her before she decides to run.

"I told you not to do that." It comes out a violent snarl and she goes stiff in my grip. My fingers find her chin and I tilt her face up so that I can look into her eyes.

"Why?" she squeaks out.

"Because if you run," I tell her, keeping my voice as easy as possible, "I will have to chase you."

I watch the pale column of her throat as she swallows.

"All right," she says breathlessly.

When her eyes flash, though, belying her words, I can't help the guttural growl that instinctively comes out of me in response. The scent of her fear shifts and my growl turns to a groan as it melts into something closer to the spicy scent of desire, overwhelming.

My fingers tighten on the soft curve of her hips and I want nothing more than to feel her tightness around me as I enter her.

"And," she draws the word out, her voice gone husky with desire. "What happens when you catch me?"

She likes the idea of it.

My entire body throbs in response.

I sink my mouth onto her skin, letting my fangs grate against the delicious expanse of her neck.

"I would mark you as mine," I tell her honestly, lifting my mouth from her face to better look at her. My fingers tighten, digging into the thick, feminine curve of her hip. "So that no male, whether of this world or another, would think that they have a chance with a woman such as you, a witch worthy of a love unconstrained by time and space."

Her pupils dilate, the scent of her arousal hanging heavy the air.

Perfect and delicate and addictive.

Just like her. *Mine.*

I lift my face from her ne towards hers. I inhale deeply,

breathing her in, unable to stop my groan of desire. Our lips are a whisper's breadth apart, and when her mouth parts in anticipation of mine, I decide I will kiss her now.

I lean down, closing the distance—when she pulls away, taking a step back.

I blink, then straighten.

Her breasts rise and fall rapidly, fetchingly, a result of her accelerated breathing.

Accelerated… because of me.

There shouldn't be distance between us. I want to hold her in my arms and feel the flutter of her heart against my rib cage.

I don't move, though. I stand stock-still, so as to avoid further frightening her. As much as I'd love to chase her, to catch her, I want even less for her to run.

Part of me understands that she needs to come to me willingly. I may not know exactly who I am, I may not have all of my memories… or any of them, but I have a feeling I'm looking at my future.

My instinct knows.

She takes another step back, the red hair tugged from her braids wild against her cheeks, stray curls tumbling down her back.

The corners of her lips turn down and I long, more than anything, to press my fingertips against their curves until she's smiling once more.

"You're not in your right mind," she says. Her gaze finally breaks from mine, and it feels as if my soul has been broken in that moment and the only way it can be repaired is to have her in my arms again.

"I'm capable of telling you what I want and what I don't want," I tell her seriously. "And I'm looking at everything I want right now."

She arches one red eyebrow at me, a challenge if I've ever seen one. I'm sure I've seen one at some point, at the very least.

"We have work to do," she announces, ignoring my declaration, but it's clear from the heat of the scent left in her wake as she turns on her heel and opens the arched door to her shop that it's only a matter of time until I get what we both want: each other.

I don't need my memories to know the truth of that.

I let myself smile.

Patience is all I need.

CHAPTER 7

WILLOW

Try as I might, I can't seem to recover my composure.

Business stays fairly steady throughout the day, giving me enough reprieve from having to look at my emotions any closer than I'd like to.

There's a rush of customers once the doors are open, and I assume the festival has wrapped up on the square. Mostly, my regulars are in for refills of their favorite balms and solutions. In some cases, medicated ointments, their own herbs, spiced salts for bathing with a variety of charmed effects: relaxation, dreamless sleep, sore muscles, or, a trickier and more expensive salt bath that causes pleasant dreams.

There are endless questions on plant care, and in one case, a request for a potion designed to help hair to grow back. I warn that particular customer that I can offer no guarantees.

However, I do have an idea for how to help, and assure him it may take several days for the potion to be ready. He seems to take heart in that, and leaves satisfied that I'll provide a solution for him.

It doesn't matter how busy we are though, not really, because Kieran looms so large in my mind.

Before long, my stomach is growling with hunger, demanding to be fed. It's well after one or two o'clock in the afternoon. I lost track of time what with the rush until my stomach was ready to remind me of my oversight.

As for Kieran, I'm grateful that the business has kept us from each other. While I handled the more complicated requests, he was careful to assist in packaging and payment and all the other bits and bobs of stocking shelves and readying customer purchases.

If the customers notice something's changed about him, they don't say it. More than one though, seem surprised by his decidedly helpful attitude. I've tried my best not to look at him, but now that it is just the two of us alone in the shop. Well, alone save for my plants and Chirp, who snoozes quietly in the corner on his favorite perch… still, it's too easy to become overly aware of Kieran.

"You're hungry," he announces, breaking the silence. There's an undercurrent to his statement that I don't quite know how to answer.

"I am hungry," I finally squeak out. He doesn't need to know that I'm hungry for more than lunch. He doesn't need to know that I've been doing my best all day to ignore just how good it felt to be called his. My cheeks heat at the mere thought and I know I'm blushing as red as the hair that coils unruly and frizzing around my temples.

He stands in the doorway between the greenhouse and the main shop, the humidity behind him causing mist to swirl around his ankles and the pointed tips of his ears. The sight makes my breath catch.

"I prepared something for you," he says breezily, as if he's been making lunch for me our entire lives. I blink, certain I misunderstood him.

"What do you mean?" I ask.

He arches an insouciant eyebrow, clearly amused by my lack of understanding.

"I've made lunch for us," he enunciates carefully.

"Right," I manage, nervous in spite of myself. "What I should have asked was, why?"

To my surprise, the cocky smile on his face grows. "I must have been an utter asshole to have you wonder why I've made us both something to eat when it's the least I can do for you." He leans heavily against the doorframe, and it's then I realize that despite his lean, well-muscled figure, he's quite large. The tips of his ears extend past the silver fall of his hair, practically brushing the top of the open archway.

My breath catches, it hitting me all over again just how handsome and compelling a figure he cuts. You'd think that I would be over it after all this time, but his beauty cuts me fresh and new, except this time there's a care behind it that doesn't leave me cold and that I fear is far more dangerous than his casual cruelty. Because when he remembers who he is, which he will, and he remembers how he feels about me, which is not how he feels about me right now, it will hurt all the more to remember how he's looking at me in this moment. A great sadness wells in my heart and I swallow hard, resisting the urge to break down in tears before him, to mourn the loss that hasn't even happened.

"Don't look like that," he cautions, closing the door behind him, the noise jolting me back to the present. "I don't like to see you sad. Is there something about lunch that upsets you?"

I sniffle, then laugh at his outrageous question.

"Of course not," I say, feeling watery still, like I might burst into tears at any moment.

"I can't stand to see a beautiful woman cry," he tells me, brushing a knuckle over my cheek. Sure enough, one traitorous tear sits on his hand and shame fills me at the sight of it twinkling in the dim afternoon light. To my surprise, he raises the knuckle to his hand, his lips brushing against where my tear rests.

"Why did you do that?" I ask, shocked out of my ridiculous, morose mess. Stupid to mourn something that will never happen.

The smirk on his lips fades and his eyes darken as he stares at me intently. A shiver goes down my back at his focus.

"Because I think I'll die," he says.

It's so unexpectedly dramatic and over the top that I can't help but burst into a peal of laughter. Laughter that turns into awkward silence when he doesn't join in. I clear my throat, unsure of how to proceed. "Maybe it would be better if I paired up with someone else—"

"I forbid it."

"Excuse me?"

"I said no," he continues. "I meant what I said at the festival this morning. You're mine. Mine to taste, mine to touch, and mine to care for, and I will not allow anyone else the pleasure and privilege of your company."

Hoo boy, I fan my face.

If he remembers, I'll almost feel sorry for him. And then I remember how he treated me and decide I might as well enjoy it.

"I feel like I need to tell you something," I say, abandoning all caution.

"Nothing you can say will dissuade me from pursuing you," he replies just as calmly as though he was foreseeing reticence on my part. I cough, completely uncomfortable and, I'm embarrassed to admit, amused.

"What if I told you you don't even like me?" It's my turn to raise my eyebrows and I relish the perfect occasion to do so, pursing my lips and waiting for a reply from the cocky fae prince. "What if I told you you could barely stand my company?" I challenge him.

He doesn't answer right away, his smile fading into some expression that makes me regret saying anything at all.

"Then I would tell you that you are sorely mistaken, because there's no way that I could be in the same room with the creature such as yourself and see all you do for the people of this town and feel anything but the utmost admiration for who you are."

My jaw drops and he has the audacity to chuck his hand under my chin, to close it for me with familiarity that leaves me just as breathless as his handsomeness.

"Now, about that lunch," he says breezily, as if he hasn't just turned my entire world upside down. There are so many things wrong with everything that he said, with all the ways that he is acting, and yet I can't bring myself to not want to believe him when he tells me something so beautiful.

"While you were speaking with the last customer, I took the liberty to go through your kitchen and assemble the best lunch that I could for you." The put-upon expression he wears is so much more familiar than the besotted one as he turns away that its sight is bittersweet.

"And what I found is that you need to take better care of yourself, Miss Willow," he says while traipsing through my hallway with the swagger of a man who thinks he owns the place. Were it anyone but Kieran under some sort of amnesia curse, I might be offended by it, but as it is, I am thoroughly amused, which might say something more about my character that I'd like to admit.

"I did the best I could do with the meager contents of your cupboard," he calls over one shoulder, and I have to bite back a laugh at how thoroughly put out he seems by my admittedly poor selection of food.

"I've been busy," I say by way of protest and he snorts in apparent disagreement.

"How do you expect to take care of anyone else if you're hardly taking care of yourself?" he asks me, swinging wide the door to my kitchen. I try to stifle my gasp but it comes out anyway, hand over my mouth, staring around wide-eyed at the spread he's managed to put together while I finished up with the customer suffering from hair loss.

My table's laden with fruits from the greenhouse arranged elegantly, strawberries sliced to resemble roses, the last pot of summer's honey sitting like a sign in a circle of yellow cheese slices. The last dregs of the ham I made a few days prior has been sliced into succulent pieces and set beside a fresh bread he must've baked between his store chores.

"Don't worry, I've closed the door, locked it, and changed the sign to say you're closed for lunch," he tells me. He seems slightly twitchier than normal, his eyes laser-focused on me, his arms crossed elegantly across his chest. It takes a moment to realize he's nervous. He wants my approval. I'm not sure how I could give him anything else.

"This is fabulous," I tell him. "No one's ever done anything like this for me."

"Well," he drawls. "That certainly makes my job easier."

How does that make your job easier?" I ask, amused and mystified. My face scrunches up as I study him trying to make heads or tails of it.

"Because that means all the idiots who came before me have set the bar so incredibly low that making you fall in love with me will hardly be difficult at all."

I stare at him, waiting for the punchline, but he simply turns around and fixes me a beautifully arranged plate and hands it to me with an entirely self-satisfied expression. This isn't right. I shake my head, gathering my thoughts, trying to deliver the news to him in a way that he can get through his thick Unseelie fae prince skull. He might be stubborn but no one's more stubborn than the willow tree. We bend in the wind, we dance with it, but we don't snap and break.

"It's not right for me to take advantage of you right now," I tell him firmly.

"Oh," he says with a satisfied look on his face. "I didn't know you wanted to take advantage of me."

I sputter, growing more annoyed by the millisecond. "You are not in your right mind," I enunciate carefully. "You don't even like me. Your normal self can hardly stand to breathe the same air as I do. You can't keep up with this. It wouldn't be fair to either one of us for you to start something with me while under a spell. It's unethical," I tack on at the last minute as he opens his mouth, looking like he's about to argue with me yet again. Not on my watch. I'm not about to take advantage of him. I'm not about to delude myself for one minute into thinking that this man, this fae, actually wants anything to do with me. It will just end up hurting us both. I suck in a breath, waiting for him to argue, preparing myself for more, but all he does is shrug his shoulders.

"If you insist," he says agreeably.

"It just wouldn't be right," I start, and then stop, pulling myself up short. I narrow my eyes at him. "What do you mean?"

"Well, if you're so bothered by the idea of me liking you and so concerned with the ethics of it, then that's fine, I'll respect that," he says, blinking his eyes carefully. I wish he wouldn't do that. He has very nice eyes, very nice everything. I heave a sigh that comes out somewhere between resignation, despair, and exhaustion.

"Eat," he says easily, "it will make you feel better."

"And you don't expect anything in return?" I ask. So what if I'm untrusting? He hasn't given me any reason to be anything otherwise. He is an Unseelie fae, after all.

He shrugs one shoulder, casual, elegant, flippant, beautiful. Hiring him was a mistake.

"I want you to feel well," he says breezily. "I want you to be able to conduct your business and not collapse while doing it."

"Hmph," I huff.

"Well, if you're this suspicious all the time," he announces, piling his own plate high with food, "no wonder no one's ever made lunch for you."

"How rude," I gasp.

He grins at me. "Tell the truth, when's the last time you let someone take care of you? When is the last time someone insisted on it?"

I want to deny the truth in his words, but they hit me like a brick to the heart, because there's truth in them. I haven't let anyone help me, I haven't let anyone get close to me. My coven sisters, yes, but I'm not sure that counts. Not in the way he means it. "When was your last lover?" he asks, his tone so casual that I'm answering before I can think better of it.

"Two years ago," I say, then blush, fresh color singeing its way into the roots of my red hair.

Dear goddess, why did I say that? As if he needed any more information about me. Why can't I keep my mouth shut around him?

"And when's the last time you brought yourself to orgasm?" he asks calmly. This time I don't answer. I have that much sense at the very least.

Unfortunately, now this is all I can think about is when the last time was that I made myself come. When was the last time I crawled under the covers and worshiped my body by myself? I frown, disgruntled because I can't remember. I've been too busy. I've been so exhausted from working so hard that I've collapsed into bed unsatisfied and exhausted most nights. He clucks his tongue, clicking softly along his fangs, and I glanced up in surprise.

"None of your business," I grid out.

"What if I want to make it my business?" he asks lightly.

"We've just agreed that nothing can come of this," I say, motioning between us.

"So you admit there is a this?" he asks slyly.

I groan in frustration, my forehead slamming against the table where I've sat.

"Why does it have to be anything?" Kieran says softly. "Why can't we just be two adult individuals who can agree to enjoy each other's company for as long as it lasts?"

Glaring at him, I stuff some bread into my mouth and chew slowly to avoid having answer his question. We eat the rest of the meal in silence because how in the world am I supposed to talk to him when he has one thing on his mind and is making the same one thing be on my mind? Not fair.

It's not exactly uncompanionable. I don't know if the tension between us is one-sided, but it's taking all of my energy not to fidget and think about what he would feel like between my thighs, to wonder what exactly being with a fae prince would be like. Wondering what exactly would happened were he never to remember how much he hates me. Wondering what it would be like to be wanted by someone that I've wanted since the moment I laid eyes on him.

And wondering what it would be like to be worthy of being his.

CHAPTER 8

KIERAN

I very nearly feel guilty now that I've decided on my plan of action.

I will convince my Willow witch that I am worthy as a bedmate and a friend, for it seems she struggles to accept either of those realities—or, more troublingly, her self-esteem is just that low.

That can't be.

I nearly dismiss the thought, because how could someone as undoubtedly wonderful as Willow have any issues with her self-confidence?

As for her notion that I despised her before the spell that has rendered me memoryless, I have an even harder time believing that. There's no world in which I could be around a female of her caliber and not fall instantly in love or, at the very least, in lust.

The day draws to a close, the amount of customers lessening the deeper the sun slinks beyond the horizon line.

The dark evergreen tops of the Elder Forest finally succeed in blotting out all of its light. Willow's long been ensconced in her laboratory, brewing a potion for the poor man desperate for hair. I take my time restocking the shelves, making sure everything is done to what I've come to understand are Willow's exacting standards.

I restock, and I plan. I need to know exactly what I will say to her when she finds I have not left for the day as she instructed.

I'm not leaving her side.

Ever.

Victory goes to the bold. So I stay, ensuring that every bit of her store is as perfect as I can possibly make it. When I'm finished, my possessiveness has me triple checking that the door is locked.

Finally, I make my way to the room where Willow brews her potions.

I pause before the door, not wishing to alarm her, knowing exactly how volatile this sort of spell work can be.

I frown, unsure how I can be so sure of it, but the truth of the thought rings out in my head like a bell.

So it is with great caution and quiet that I finally tug the door to Willow's laboratory open.

My breath catches, and I look my fill.

Her hair spirals in angelic curls around her fair face. The light from the fire under the cauldron illuminates her like some storybook creature, a goddess the likes of which mere fae or mortals could not capture in ink no matter their skill.

The heat of the room washes over me just as I notice the sheen of glistening sweat along the generous curves of her breasts, as if beckoning me for a taste.

I couldn't look away if I tried. I wouldn't want to.

Willow pays no notice me, too involved in murmuring the incantations and adding handfuls of fresh herbs and plant material to the steaming cauldron in front of her. She's reflected infinitely in the bottles and glazed vases lining the shelves of the arched windows behind her.

The view frames her deliciously ample bottom. All of her, in fact. Every perfect curve, every breath captured and refracted back on itself hundreds and hundreds of times. It's nearly overwhelming and my breath catches as fresh desire unspools through me.

I can't imagine a more beautiful sight than this little female hard at work, the fruits of her labor filling the air with the tang of magic and her perfection bathed in light from the fire of the cauldron.

Her brow furrows in concentration, the lush pink of her lips a thin line. It irks me to see that she is displeased with her efforts. I don't remember much, but I think I'd remember if I'd met someone with such a bent towards perfection as my Willow.

My mouth is moving before I have fully thought the words that they form: "Tell me how to help and I will," I say, my voice tinged with a desperation that doesn't quite surprise me.

Her hands tremble and she lets out a startled gasp. I berate myself for a moment.

I forgot Willow doesn't have the same preternatural hearing as I do.

Charmingly, she doesn't answer right away, but goes back to decanting whatever substance trickles into the cauldron from the crystal flagon in her hand.

It hisses faintly as it reaches its destination.

"Oh, you don't have to. I know you're tired after today, you've done so much already."

"It would be my pleasure," I tell her. "Just tell me what it is you require."

She fidgets, her nose twitching, and from the way she shifts her weight, I can tell that she's incredibly uncomfortable. One look at the red curl tickling her nose tells me exactly what she needs without her having to say word.

"I'm going to sneeze," she pronounces quietly, determination etched in the lines of her face. "If I disrupt the flow of this rosemary tincture, the whole batch might be ruined." Her voice trembles, her nostrils twitching.

"I have you," I tell her, supremely confident in my ability to at least help with this task. I'm behind her in a flash. Despite the acrid smell of the brew she's working on, I can still scent the incredible perfume of her body on the air, and it takes all of my self-control not to lose sight of what she needs.

I don't want to startle her and cause her to ruin her work; I don't want to be so rough with her, but she pours from the flagon too quickly.

With as much tender care as I can muster, I gently comb my fingers around the skin of her neck, the pads stroking against her cheeks as I carefully pull the glory of her fiery hair out of her face.

She doesn't say a word, though her breath seems to fall and rise more rapidly even as she steadily pours the tincture into the hissing cauldron.

From this place behind her, my hands tangled in the unruly mess of her red hair, I have the most perfect view of her cleavage, which wobbles enticingly with every shaky breath. It's easy to imagine the shape of her breasts under the tight lines of her dress. It's easy to imagine what she would feel like beneath me were we in a different position, would I be so lucky to be afforded such a miracle. I can't help myself, I lean down, closing my eyes and breathing her in.

Perfection.

When I open my eyes, goosebumps have pebbled across the nape of her neck and her shoulders and satisfaction closes around me, much like the steam from the cauldron. It is not the scent of fear, or the potion merrily bubbling under her skillful watch… but the smell of a woman with one thing on her mind.

Lucky for me, it's the exact thing that's on my mind too.

Lust.

Desire.

Sex.

A rasping chuckle comes out of me. Her hands tremble as she replaces the stopper on the crystal vial and sets it aside.

"What—what is so funny?" she asks. Her voice is deliciously hoarse, and I love that I've caused the shift in her speech— and in the scent and carriage of her body.

I caused that.

"Because no matter what your voice tells me," I murmur to her soothingly, my lips brushing against the delectable shell of her ear, pink flushing up the nape of her neck beneath the goosebumps. "I can scent your cunt's readiness to take me."

CHAPTER 9

WILLOW

I fear my heart, beating louder than any drum I've ever heard, may simply take flight like a bird and burst through the cage of my body.

Of all the things I expected Kieran might say, telling me he could smell *me* and my *arousal* was not one of them.

What's worse is that I can't call him a liar because from the moment his skin touched mine, wanting more was about the only thing I could think of. Wanting to feel the electric caress of his fingers against more than my neck, and more interesting and varied places than my cheeks, was about all I could focus on.

Lucky for me, I have morals. Morals which tell me that taking him up on his very enticing offer would be very wrong.

"The caudron smoke must be addling your head," I tell him politely.

He huffs a laugh and tightens his grip on my hair.

"I see you insist on continuing this game of ours," he says smoothly. His grip loosens, but only infinitesimally.

The only reason I'm aware of it at all is because my body's never been so aware of everything all at once.

I try to pull away, but his hand wraps around the nape of my neck. I'm pulled me back to him before I make any progress with that particular goal. Wetness seeps between my legs and I make an embarrassingly soft mewling noise.

"The thing is, my Willow witch..." His lips brush against my neck and I arch into him, the soft curve of my ass pressed against the hardness in his pants. Hardness that I'm suddenly even more interested in.

I very much like everything that he is doing at this very moment.

He knows it, too. I'm not sure I like that, at least.

"The thing is, you overestimate my patience, and you underestimate how much I enjoy playing a game when the prize is already right in front of me."

His fangs scrape against the place where my neck meets my shoulder, and there's no denying the need in the desperate moan that escapes me now. His breath tickles my skin when he laughs, his teeth pressing harder into me, the length of him somehow growing harder and larger than even before.

Goddess.

He must be massive. I whimper as his arm circles my waist, strong hand finding my breast.

"Will you lie to me, my Willow?" he asks, his voice all but a growl against my skin. The pressure of his teeth, of his body, increasing the longer he holds me like this.

I don't want him to let me go.

"Will you tell me that you are thinking of someone else? That it's not me that you're responding to so perfectly in my arms, at this very moment?"

There's an unhinged ferocity in the questions that I've never heard from him before. Every inch of me heats in response to the possessive edge around it.

Who would have thought I wanted to be man-handled?

Or would it be fae-handled?

"Are you trying to think of the words that will best deceive me, Willow?"

"I'm trying to think of the ones that will best deceive myself," I mutter, then wriggle away from him.

Or, at least, I try to, but only succeed in making us both groan as I unwittingly rub against the huge, hard press of his cock.

"Why deceive either one of us?" he asks, and I shudder as his tongue flicks out, tasting the slight shimmer of sweat on my neck.

"Because I have work to do," I force out, finally extricating myself from his grip.

Which basically leaves me bereft and panting with need.

How wonderful.

It's not a lie though. I have a ton to do.

"What work is more important than feeling good?" he asks, and there's no censure in the question, or angry aggression, which I might have guessed at based on my little experience with other men—instead, he sounds amused.

Amused!

I glance over my shoulder at him, straighten the bodice of my overdress, and clear my throat in a way that means I'm very serious.

I frown for extra serious impact as I inspect his expression for proof of my suspicions.

Sure enough, there's a slight smile quirking up the corners of his mouth.

"Work that makes sure my clients keep feeling well. It's not all hair potions." Now truly irritated, I push myself away from his wandering hands tempting me to all sorts of trouble and jerk my chin towards the lye solution I have setting up in a huge glass mixing bowl. "See that? I have to make soap, too. That lye won't keep forever."

It's not quite true, but he doesn't need to know that.

When I chance another furtive glance at him, he's frowning now, too.

Good.

"Soap?" He raises both eyebrows, his beetle wings rattling slightly behind him in what I can only suppose is complete bemusement.

"Soap," I agree, nodding sagely, hoping the scents of the lye solution and the cauldron bubbling are overriding what he can surely smell from my skin.

He's made it all too clear that it's harder to lie to someone with an excellent sense of smell than I'd like it to be.

"I don't know anything about soap," he says, and the carnal, heavy look in his gaze turns lighter, curiosity sparking in his expression.

A smile of my own kicks my lips up because, frankly, it's darling to see him light up like a bright star at the idea of learning something new.

"Why can't they make their own soap? What's special about this one?"

Carefully, I tug on the dragon skin gloves I reserve for handing volatile materials and begin ladling the hair tonic into the waiting jars.

"This soap is one of my best sellers, and I'm nearly out. The reason they can't make their own is because, for one, it's a secret recipe that uses a special blend of oils especially formulated for dry, sensitive skin," I state, narrowing my eyes and daring the potion to go anywhere but where I want it.

"And secondly?" Kieran asks, taking the freshly decanted potion and handing me an empty bottle.

"Secondly, the only place the ingredients are grown for it in a three-hundred-mile radius is in my greenhouse." The potion is already beginning to congeal, and while it won't ever solidify fully, the less liquid it becomes, the harder it is to pour into the little glass bottles. I frown, biting my lower lip, and Kieran wordlessly assists, anticipating the moment I'll need a fresh bottle until I'm scraping the last of the potion out of the cauldron.

"Phew." I tug the dragon gloves off, wiping the sweat beading at my brow. "Thank you," I tell him simply, replacing the gloves on their hook at the side of the table. "That was much easier with your help."

"There are so many things I could make easier for you, would you let me," he murmurs, that heavy-lidded look in his eyes again, the one that promises a night of no sleep.

"Right," I say brightly. "Lye will burn your skin right off, so you'll want to handle it with gloves of your own, glasses for safety, and a thick apron."

"Burn my skin off?" he repeats, blinking slowly.

"To the bone, if you let it." I grin manically at him, pleased at my violent segue.

"Vile," he says agreeably, then takes the dragon skin gloves from their hook and holds them out to me. "You'll want these again. I assume you took them off because you simply can't live without touching me."

My mouth drops open, and he tips his head back and lets out a laugh, his wings stretching out full behind him for a brief, glorious second.

It takes me too long to get a grip on myself, during which time he's grinning at me like a cat with a canary.

Chirp hoots softly from his perch on the door, and it feels like they're in cahoots, laughing at me.

"Thank you," I tell him primly, snatching the gloves out of his hands.

Or, at least, I attempt to, but he tsks at me, not letting go of them.

My brow furrows.

"You can at least let me help you put them back on," he says silkily. He slowly pulls open the glove, and when I look up at him, all I see on his face is unfettered desire.

I swallow, knowing all too well my damnably pale skin is giving away just how flushed and hot I feel, and knowing he knows.

Which I also know is a problem.

Really, it's a lot of knowing.

I would rather just turn off my brain and not know, but here I am, knowing too much and knowing this won't end well.

So I thrust my hand inside the glove as fast as possible, then snatch its mate away from him and tug it on myself.

He sniffs, sounding put out, but when I dare to glance at him again, his shoulders are shaking from suppressing a laugh.

"You really are the most stubborn witch, aren't you?"

"Yes," I tell him. "Now let's make some soap."

"Why?" The syllable is a purr, velvet-smooth against my senses.

Sadly for both of us, I'm stubborn *and* I'm very good at ignoring my senses.

"Are you thinking dirty thoughts? Is that why you're so fixated on soap?"

"I'm fixated on soap because it's my job, which provides the roof over my head, and yours, actually," I tell him, lust turning into annoyance so fast I suspect I may have whiplash later. And not just in my neck.

Can you get whiplash in your babymaker?

I might sell potions for all sorts of ailments, but I can't say I have one for that.

Huffing, I continue. "Not all of us were born princes with a silver spoon in our mouths."

Instead of looking annoyed, as I intended, Kieran has the audacity to simply look more amused. "I should hope not. That would make for an incredibly boring world, and quite too many silver spoons. I have to say, I much prefer the idea of you being a princess to being another prince. Nothing wrong with the other, I simply adore the idea of sinking to the hilt into your slick heat."

I goggle at him, lye solution near forgotten on the counter behind me as I process his words, but he's not done.

"Also, how is one born with a spoon in their mouth? Is this some witchy ritual I know nothing of?"

"Ugh, of course it's not, it's just an expression—"

He's laughing at me again, that musical, dark melody erupting from his lips and sending fresh goosebumps down my spine. It's such an infectious sound that I find myself grinning back up at him, a laugh threatening to come out of my own mouth like laughing with him is the most natural thing in the world.

What if it is?

What if this little glimpse into who he is under the hard shell of his constructed identity, free of the pressure of past and present expectations, is the real Kieran?

What if laughing with him is what I am supposed to be doing?

My heart skips a beat, and it must show on my face because the sound of his laugh softens into something else, something caught between a groan and a sigh.

I want to kiss him.

I want to feel his mouth against mine, to taste that noise and all the other ones he'll make as I wrap myself around him.

My feet take a step back. And another, until I'm pressed up against the wall of shelving, chock full of ingredients.

Ingredients I haven't put away or organized or labeled yet, because all my plans went ass over tea kettle what with ye olde Elder Gods and an amnesiac fae prince.

Suddenly, I'm not interested in kissing Kieran.

Or in making the soap.

I'm bone tired, and it's hit me like a fifty-pound sack of manure swung off the back of the delivery cart.

The potion for my customer has been made and decanted, and I sag against the shelves, my eyes fluttering closed.

"You need sleep," Kieran says, the words laced with commanding imperiousness.

"I need to use the lye mixture," I tell him, opening my eyes and narrowing them at His Majesty of the Underhill.

Or whatever the honorific would be for an exiled Unseelie.

How should I know? I'm a lowly human witch, one he never deigned to worry about when he had his memories.

"I will do it for you."

It's a sign of how completely done with this day I am that I even consider it.

"It would be my honor to do it for you," he adds sincerely, and I pinch the bridge of my nose in annoyance.

"Have you a lot of soap-making experience?" I ask him, incredulous and prickly all at once. "Have you been holding out on me?"

"I was known as the royal soap maker in Unseelie court." He sweeps into a low bow, the muscles under his tight-stretched shirt rippling.

I blink at him. "What? Really?"

He unfolds from the waist, leaning against the scarred wooden worktable and bestowing me with a grin only capable of being described as feral. "No."

I scoff and roll my eyes, but he slaps a palm against the table, startling me back to attention.

"I am willing to learn, Willow, and I am sure you can point me to a recipe. If I know anything about you, it's that you are hard-pressed to let a good recipe or note or thought go unwritten."

I tilt my head because, while he's not wrong, he shouldn't know that. "Did you remember that? Is it coming back?"

He tips his face back and laughs, then raises a hand to gesture at the overflowing leather-bound grimoire I've stuffed full of all the things he just accused me of loving to write.

My cheeks pink. "If you mess up the recipe, I'll have to buy new supplies," I manage.

"I fully expect you to dock the supplies from my pay."

"Of course I wouldn't!" I gasp, scandalized. "Losing supplies is part of training an apprentice."

His gaze sears through me and I swallow, fully aware I have my back against the wall.

Literally.

My half-empty shelves are keeping me from putting any more room between us.

"Now I'm your apprentice, am I?" He all but purrs the question.

"Of course you are," I say, drawing myself up to my full height.

Which is not very impressive. At all.

Especially compared to a prince of the Unseelie, who looms larger than life even next to the tallest of mortals.

How would sex even work between us? There's no way he would fit.

Dear goddess.

I blanch and decide I'm totally and irrevocably done with this day, because that's an errant thought that should never have been shaken loose.

"The recipe is in the grimoire. You may need ingredients that haven't been labeled and restocked yet. It's on my—"

"To-do list," he finishes for me.

I try to scowl, but end up smiling anyway. "Yes. On my to-do list. Please be careful. The gloves and—"

"Safety glasses are hanging on the table." He raises an amused eyebrow. "I had no idea you cared so much for my physical safety."

I bite back a sour reply about his physical safety and instead paste a weary smile on my face. "Be careful," I tell him. "Read the directions twice before beginning. The lye solution will burn."

"Does this need any magical charms or incantations?" he asks, and there is a slight pinch of worry between his brows that melts my heart. Just a little.

"No," I tell him. "This is just soap. If it needs charming, I do it during the four- to six-week curing period."

Relief washes the wrinkle in his forehead away, and it's so charming that I melt a little bit more.

"Don't stay up too late," I finally manage, extricating myself from the shelves and doing my best to slither past his tall, lean frame and through the door.

"I wouldn't dream of it. I will, however, say that I hope you dream of me." He utters it in a low, delicious rumble that makes my entire body tighten with desire.

And for the first time in my life, I can't get out of my apothecary laboratory fast enough.

CHAPTER 10

WILLOW

I wake to an empty bed.

Chirp is nowhere to be seen, my owl familiar likely off hunting or stretching his wings before the sun fully hangs in the near-winter sky.

Kieran isn't here either, and I tell myself I'm grateful I don't have to deal with his warm, strong body stretched out next to mine.

Definitely grateful. Relieved. That, too.

Mm-hmm.

The window shows an expanse of thick, pregnant gray clouds, and I frown at the crust of frost lining the sill.

It's too early for snow.

At least, it should be.

It's unusual for us to see snow here before the new year. Not impossible, but improbable.

I sit up, rubbing at my eyes and not quite believing the sight just outside the panes of glass. Grackles flit about over the frosted outlines of fallen leaves, and cold washes over me as a strong wind buffets the house.

Winter, it seems, has decided to breathe upon Wild Oak Woods early.

My frown deepens as I slide out of my warm bed, my toes chilling the moment they leave the threadbare rug and hit the wood planks.

Where is Kieran?

Washing up is going to be brisk today—the need to make sure my accidental house guest hasn't gotten into trouble takes precedence over how much I want a nice, long soak in the tub.

Sighing, I disrobe quickly, settling on using the wash basin as fast as possible and then going to hunt for my royal pain of an apprentice.

Water slides from the mouth of the pitcher into the floral ceramic basin, the enchantment on the rim causing the flowers wreathing it to bloom as the bowl fills. The charmed flowers release a lovely, fresh scent as they open, perfuming the water and the air as I wash up.

My red curls stick out at every impossible angle, and I tsk at my reflection in frustration as I run my fingers through it in an attempt to tame my mane into something less wild. I release an annoyed huff of breath and give up, raking it back into an impressively mussed topknot, and splash icy water all over myself before vigorously rubbing down all my important bits.

Teeth are next, and I tell myself that I always spend an inordinate amount of time brushing them, and that my desire for cleanliness has nothing to do with my desire for Kieran.

A soft hoot interrupts my internal lies, and I rush to put on my favorite pair of thick fleece-lined trousers, high wool socks knitted in shades of pink. The softest shirt I own tucks into the tops of the pants, and I fasten my well-worn leather suspenders over my shoulders and throw a bulky knit sweater over the whole ensemble.

There.

Not in the least appealing, I decide upon looking at myself in the mirror again.

The scowl really rounds things out, too.

He'll remember he's not attracted to me in no time at this rate.

A kernel of worry roots deep in my heart, because other than Chirp softly clawing at his perch in the hall, there's no sound from the rest of my house and shop.

"Maybe the wind is masking it," I tell myself, tugging my warmest boots over the lurid pink socks.

My stomach rumbles, and I realize in my exhaustion last night I didn't eat, simply collapsing into bed in lieu of anything resembling a nighttime ritual.

I scrub a palm over my freshly washed face and grimace before throwing open the door, half expecting to find Kieran curled up on the floor of the hallway like an unwelcome cat who's made himself at home.

The hall is empty, save for Chirp, who softly hoots and lands on the thick cream sweater over my shoulder.

A fresh blast of wind rattles the lead-paned windows, and I glance out them with an equally fresh wave of concern.

"What is going on with this weather?" I murmur, tugging at a loose curl before shoving it behind my ear.

I don't like it.

My plants in the greenhouse should be fine, but half my outdoor garden hasn't gone fully dormant yet. I make a mental note to cover everything as best I can, and sing some lullabies to soothe the perennials into their winter sleep.

"Where is Kieran?" I ask, fumbling through the door to my laboratory, because there is no way he's still in here. The soap recipe should have set up within an hour, even if it took him much longer to make it than me.

The laboratory is empty, but that's not what brings me up short.

There are nine loaves of soap curing on the table, three different kinds. Stunned, I marvel at them. The tops aren't as neat as mine would be, but they're perfectly acceptable. There's no soap ash either, which means that not only did Kieran execute all three soap recipes correctly, he read my personal notes on ensuring the loaves would be as pretty for display as he could manage.

Tears threaten, stinging my eyes, and all my resolve to be annoyed with him simply vanishes.

This isn't something I expected him to do; to simply tackle all the soap-making on my extensive to-do list, nor to do it carefully and well. It's not something anyone who just wanted to have sex with me would do.

It's thoughtful. It's caring, and it's kind.

And it's going to take all of my willpower to keep the male at arm's length, because goddess, does it feel wonderful to have someone do something so thoughtful for me.

I sniffle, wiping the back of my hand over my now-wet lashes, some of the pressure that's dogged my steps for days finally alleviated.

My gaze lifts from the lovely assortment of soaps curing on the otherwise tidy worktable to the shelves that need to be restocked today.

Any remaining breath leaves my lungs, and my jaw drops.

They've been restocked.

Every ingredient sits in a perfectly straight row.

My boots tick-tick against the flagstone floor as I try to make sense of the sight before me. It's all done perfectly. Flawless.

Each crystal vial and glass bottle has been tagged with twine.

"There's an updated inventory sheet, too." Kieran's voice is a low, tired rumble, and I startle at the unexpected sound.

I swivel on the ball of my foot only to find him directly

behind me, his brilliant wings extended fully behind him, half-moon circles under his eyes.

"Why?" My voice breaks on the word. "How? Did you stay up all night?"

"Because you needed help." He shrugs one shoulder, as if it's the most obvious thing in the world. "And because I could give it to you. I would give you much more if you let me." His big, warm hands bracket my upper arms and I tilt my chin up to him, not caring that tears are now openly streaming down my cheeks.

It seems cruel, this twist of fate, to give me the illusion everything I've ever wanted from a partner is in the male I want as a partner, only for it to be the result of some wayward spell.

"You don't mean that," I tell him, and it doesn't come off as mean or callous as I'd like.

It doesn't sound mean or callous at all. It sounds wretched, like I've been laid bare and vulnerable before him. Exactly as I feel on the inside.

His gaze darts between my eyes, as if he doesn't know where to look, as if I've exposed myself to him and it's too much.

It's too much for me.

"I do mean that."

I wriggle out of his grasp, trying to hold onto my own reality in lieu of his hands, and march around to the doorway again. Chirp nibbles at my earlobe in solidarity.

"Why can't you believe that I want you? Want all of you?" This time, his voice breaks, and the sound hurts me.

I rub the ache in my chest.

"Because you're under a spell, Kieran. You don't... you don't even like me."

"You've said that over and over again," he says fiercely, his wings buzzing behind him. "You've said it so often that it sounds more false every time you do. I just don't know if you're lying to yourself or if I was lying to both of us. Because there is no world in which I could be in the same place as you, breathe the same air as you, and not need you. Not want you. You are..." He pauses, his nostrils flaring as he inhales. "You are special."

The strange, strangled way he says the word confuses me.

Because it doesn't sound like it fits. It doesn't sound like it's what he meant to say at all.

My stomach growls.

"Did you sleep at all?" I ask him, changing the subject.

His wings buzz louder, but to his benefit, he doesn't call out the fact I'm a coward, that I'm deathly afraid of whatever is happening between the two of us.

He doesn't have to, though; it's in the way he studies me, with a slight downward tilt to his chin. Kieran's disappointed in me, and I hate it.

I hate disappointing people.

I hate how important disappointing him is while he's under a spell.

Isn't it?

"I don't need as much sleep as you do," he finally answers. "You need food."

He gestures for me to leave the lab and meekly, I do, ashamed and on edge as we walk in tense silence to my kitchen...

An inelegant noise climbs from my mouth.

"Was that you or Chirp?" Kieran asks, huffing out a laugh.

I toss my hair, or try to, except I've forgotten it's in a bun. I manage to stretch an arm up and fake a yawn, like I'm stretching and not just completely flustered about everything in my life at this moment.

Like the breakfast spread Kieran made while I slept in: scones and clotted cream and raspberry preserves. Thick, pillowy biscuits studded with dried fruit and nuts, a rasher of spiced sausages. Fresh fruit cut into shapes that mimic the fall night sky, apples in the shape of stars and pears shaped like crescent moons.

"I hope you're hungry," he says in a low voice, his lips brushing against my ear.

"This is too much," I tell him, tears threatening all over again. "You can't just come in here and—"

"And make you breakfast? I can't make you breakfast?" he interrupts again.

I narrow my eyes at him. "Exactly."

He snorts, then rolls his eyes. "Too late and too bad."

"You should have slept," I insist as he pulls a chair out for me. The admonition sounds weaker even to my ears, but he has the decency not to laugh, just smiles softly down at me, one wing brushing my shoulder as he sits next to me.

"I am fine."

"You should have at least gone back to the inn, you know?"

"Willow." He emphasizes each syllable of my name, glaring at me over a plate he continues to fill with food before setting it in front of me. "Did you forget that we are supposed to stay together while the threat from the Elder Gods and wild magic persists? Or are you still considering throwing yourself at their… mercy?"

He spits out the word mercy as though it's toxic, and I'm inclined to agree.

"I just want you to be comfortable," I argue, resigned to the fact I'm not going to win this argument and yet still unwilling to give it up. I dip a knife into the raspberry preserves.

"I cannot possibly be comfortable if for one second I think my mate could be in danger."

"I'm not in danger—" My knife clatters onto my plate. "Your *what?!*"

He sighs with great gusto, rolling his pretty pale purple eyes up to the ceiling before rolling his shirt sleeve back to his elbow. A dark aubergine marking snakes up from his wrist, the botanical design as improbable as his word choice.

I flush, all my thoughts at a complete standstill, all my arguments totally forgotten.

The leaves that wind across his lavender skin are no ordinary vines—they're the unmistakable boughs of a willow tree, dripping down his forearm like they've always been there.

"So now you see."

I stuff a scone into my mouth as fast as I can, trying to buy time to think.

Unfortunately, all my mental faculties seem to be completely exhausted.

"Willow, I am yours." He sinks to one knee beside me, his eyes beseeching, his voice desperate.

I chew slowly, crumbs spraying out over him.

Which, unfortunately, does nothing to deter him.

"I am yours, and you are mine. I would wait forever for you to acknowledge me, to taste you on my lips again, for you to claim me as your own. I would not rush you, but know that I will not give up my pursuit of you so easily. This mark," he holds his arm up, thrusting the evidence directly into my line of sight, "this mark means that my mate has been found. And do you know when it appeared?"

I don't know, and my mouth is full, so I simply shake my head and try to have one (1) coherent thought.

And fail miserably, all thoughts scattering at the light touch of his palm upon my cheek.

"It appeared the moment I scooped you up in my arms and brought you back here. You are my mate, the only one for me, my Willow, and I will not give you up for some Elder God. And I will not be leaving your side, even if it means I have to sleep on your floors to guard you for the rest of your days." The words are fervent and powerful, and there's no hint of humor on his face, just grim determination.

"I don't understand," I finally manage, though the words just come out garbled from scone.

He laughs, a gentle smile on his face, petting my hand before he stands and pours me a steaming cup of water, my favorite loose-leaf tea already in the strainer in the fine porcelain set.

"Ginger chamomile," I say, shaking my head in disbelief.

"Your favorite." He tilts his head, pleasure clear on his face. "It was easy to tell which you preferred."

A minute ticks by, then another, the only sounds the thud of my heart in my chest and the howling of the wind outside. Even Chirp stays oddly quiet.

We gaze at each other until the silence between us is unbearable.

"I don't know what to say."

"You don't have to say anything. I am yours, and you are mine. Once you realize that, all will be well."

"But the spell. Your memory—"

He thrusts his arm down. "Memory has nothing on a mate bond, Willow. This is fate. My memory—"

"Or lack thereof," I mutter.

Kieran raises an eyebrow before continuing. "… has nothing to do with it. If I truly… if I was as awful as you say I was towards you, then all I can imagine is that I was trying to protect you."

"Or yourself," I say, my voice rising, surprising us both. "I'm hardly royal. I'm not even a fae."

"Fate does not care. Neither do I." The declaration comes out crisp and final, and I find myself blinking in surprise.

"You don't care if I fit into your life?"

"My life before is gone. My memories of it too, apparently. I have no desire to return to the Underhill."

"But you might," I tell him.

"No," he says, spreading his hands across the dining table, leaning heavily on it.

I follow his gaze to the dusty mauve flower-studded wallpaper that hangs on the upper half of the wall, the light wood board and batten, and the cupboards I've done my best to take care of, and frankly, all I see is home. Nothing magnificent or royal or fabulous or immortal, like what he must have been used to.

"You might," I mutter, feeling mutinous, trapped, and altogether unlike anything I've ever dealt with.

When he slams his hand onto the table I startle, and stare up at him with wide, disbelieving eyes. "Just because I've lost my memory doesn't mean I lost my faculty to make decisions. And where you're concerned, Willow of Wild Oak Woods, I am wholly ready to make any decision necessary to stay by your side."

I want to glare at him, to scowl and frown and continue to argue, to tell him that there's no good that can come from any attempt to pursue a relationship while he doesn't have his memories, but I find that I want to believe him. I want to believe him so much that it hurts. A physical ache deep in my bones, deep in my heart, accompanied by awareness that says I'm sure to get my heart broken. But maybe, just maybe, I want to live inside his fantasy while I can grab it—any chance of happiness—with both hands, to catch it and hold it close to my chest so that it doesn't stand a chance at getting away.

My gaze traces the path of the flowers printed on the wallpaper and I swallow, then take a careful sip of the still steaming tea before me.

Kieran is watching me with careful eyes, like he's waiting for me to argue some more, like he expects me to resist. I must be one of the most unpleasant people in the world because knowing that that's his expectation immediately makes me want to be more agreeable, simply to spite him.

"Fine."

His eyebrows rise, practically disappearing in the silver luster of his hair.

"What do you mean, fine?"

I cross my arms over my chest in spite of my resolution not to argue. "Exactly what I said. If you are determined on being my mate, then fine."

I would've thought it impossible for his eyes narrow further, but he manages. And still, he's one of the most beautiful things I've ever seen, all high cheekbones and lovely lavender skin, pointed ears, and strong muscles. The reality of what he's telling me crashes through my thick skull. He thinks we're mates. He thinks that fate has brought us together, and judging by the fresh mark on his arm, there might be more truth to his allegations than I can stand to admit.

"So you're not kicking me out?"

My hand flies to my chest, my jaw dropping open with indignation.

"Of course I'm not kicking you out, we're supposed to stay together. Or did you forget that too, just like you forgot how you can't stand me?"

He gives me a long look and I roll my shoulders, sagging and defeated, against the back of my chair. My hands fly to the thin porcelain of my teacup and I hold it in my hands not only to warm them up but as some sort of ridiculous barrier between the two of us.

"I wouldn't have left anyway," he says and he sinks into the chair next to mine. "I already told you as much."

"I don't want to fight." I shake my head. I should be ecstatic. Instead, all I feel is a sense of bone-tiredness and the certainty that soon, the other shoe will drop. Kieran will remember why it is exactly he's been so cold to me, though I have no idea what the reason is, and the thought of getting my hopes up just to have them dashed nauseates me so much that I relinquish when his hands grip on the porcelain teacup then push the plate in front of me away.

"Do not look so sad," he tells me, his brows creasing as he gives me a thorough once over. "I must've been truly horrible for you to react thusly to this news, or would you rather be wedded to one of the Elder Gods?"

I can't help but laugh at that, tipping my chin back and

studying one of the many water stains on the ceiling. I've tried painting over them several times to no avail.

"I would've thought you would be pleased by this news, considering how deliciously the sin of your arousal perfumes the air every time I touch you," he says smoothly.

I sputter in indignation, not able to get a word out edgewise before he continues.

"I assumed that some strange sense of human or witch propriety kept you from acting on your clear desires, and now that fate has revealed you to be mine, you would be gleeful at the news." He reaches for a piece of bacon and chews it as nonchalantly as is possible after one makes that sort of declaration. I stare at him, caught between annoyance and the realization that he is completely correct.

Kieran simply grins at me.

I take another bite of scone, this time smothered in clotted cream, to keep from answering.

"I always would have been a willing participant in any sexual fantasies about me you may be harboring, but now you can explore them knowing full well I would be loath to leave you afterwards." He cocked his head at me "...Is that not what you were worried about?"

Chew, chew, chew.

Swallow.

Take another bite.

Avoid the question.

"These are really quite delicious," I tell him through a full mouth.

Half his mouth kicks up at the corner, a smile that sends fresh warmth through me.

Him leaving or breaking my heart hasn't been what I was worried about, not really. He might have, yes, but that's not what's held me back.

It's that I didn't want to take advantage of the fact that his missing memories have led to a bizarre and unlikely fascination with me.

I prop my elbows on the table, well aware of how ill-mannered that is, and sink my face into them, breathing as slowly as possible.

"Are you unwell?" Kieran asks, worry clear in the words.

"Just trying to think."

"Ah."

"Ah," I echo, the sound trapped between my sleeves.

I inhale slowly, breathing in the many mouth-watering scents of the spread in front of me, the lavender I use to wash my linens, and the faint herbal scent of my own magic.

"Tell me you aren't still thinking of running off to the Elder Gods," Kieran says, and his voice breaks on the last word.

"No." My response is immediate, and fervent, and surprises us both.

His hand wraps around mine, first one and then the other, until both of mine are caged in warm lilac flesh.

"Then you'll stay with me," he presses.

I never thought before that time had mass, that it was something besides the ticking of a clock or the sun moving across the skies.

But with his gaze searching mine, his body leaning towards me, the future weighs heavy on my shoulders, heavier even than the pull of the past.

Our past—the one where I've pined after him for weeks only to be met with ice—and my past—where I've always been the one overlooked or worse, an afterthought to any partner I wanted.

His hands squeeze mine, but it's the slight tremble in them that urges me to speak, to break the spell of what was and what might be for what is, right now.

"I'll stay."

"You'll stay," he echoes, and a slow smile transforms his face, the warmth enough to melt snow in winter.

I shrug a shoulder, trying to deny my own pleasure at seeing it, at the absurdity of all of it. "I live here."

"So you do," he says, and for a second, I worry I've hurt his feelings.

I raise an eyebrow.

"So you do," he repeats, and a spark of mischief lights in his eyes that washes my worry away. "We have things to do today, people to see," he continues. "I've already tended to your more sensitive plants in the greenhouse, as well as made all the soap that you had listed in your soap-to-make list."

"Are you trying to put me out of a job?" I ask, half teasing. Or aiming for it, at least. It comes out slightly brittle, though. With too much pressure, the question would fissure and crack like too-thin ice.

Over thirty years of not feeling good enough. Of feeling like the things I do, the magic I have, my entire life's work is a simple matter of sunshine and water and time. Things an Unseelie fae prince could do without a second thought.

Things any witch with an inclination could do without so much as trying.

I swallow, trying to push the ugly thoughts back, trying to shove them back into a box and lock them away until I have the energy to pull them out and find all the holes in them.

"Never." He stands up, then leans down, close enough it feels like he's thinking of kissing me.

Or, maybe, *I'm* simply thinking of kissing *him*. My core tightens, the ever-present heat his mere existence seems to conjure spreading like wildfire, fanned to new heights by his proximity.

"You are special, Willow of Wild Oak Woods, and not just to me. You are special because you are you, a fierce, ungovernable force of nature, whose love of all things natural and green speaks to her wild heart."

My mouth pops open in surprise, my eyes widening, and this

time, the heat that explodes through me has less to do with lust than joy at feeling seen.

At the truth in his ferocious words.

Even if Kieran doesn't remember his past—he sees me. He sees who I am, and who I want to be, the witch who hides inside her greenhouse coaxing leaves to unfurl and blossoms to bloom.

Now he's the one coaxing me to do so, too.

This is real. Whatever happened to Kieran to have him lose his memories... I don't understand it, but this moment now, this man in front of me—this is more real than anything he's shown me before.

I'm moving without thinking, responding to all the hope and desire I've caged inside me, bundled up and smushed down until it threatened to explode out of me.

My lips brush against his, and my eyelids flutter shut.

It's the barest of contact, and yet my breath catches in my chest, agonizing and wonderful all at once.

I want more.

CHAPTER 11

KIERAN

Her lips are on mine and all I can do is breathe. Breathe through the aching need to pull her to me, nestle her lush curves into mine, pull her flush with me and mingle our bodies and souls.

My heart beats erratically, everything I want sitting in a rustic wooden chair in front of me wearing linen pants and raspberry-stained lips.

"Willow," I murmur. "I would put you on this very table and strip you bare, spread your legs and eat you like my own personal feast."

Her breath rushes out of her in surprise, and I fist my hands into the waist of her blouse. "I would make you see stars on the ceiling of this house, I would etch my name upon your heart and give you pleasure like you've never known."

A small moan slips from her mouth, and then her fingers slip over my cheeks, holding me steady between her hands.

"Willow." Her name is an incantation, an entreaty.

"Yes," she says, her gaze darting between my eyes. "Yes."

I don't know what she's saying yes to, not exactly, but when she presses her mouth against mine, I decide I would be an idiot to stop her kissing me and clarify.

I'll have to figure out what that yes means as we go.

Her mouth tastes like tea and honey, and every sip from her is delicious. Willow kisses me hard, her mouth parting over mine and inviting me in.

My hands go to the soft round of her waist, and I pull her off her chair until she's straddling me on the floor of her snug kitchen.

Like it's the most natural thing in the world, for us to be kissing on the floor. My cock hardens in my pants, and she lets out a whimper as it lines up with her center.

I cradle the back of her head, running an exalting hand up her side, unable to stop myself from cupping the generous breast underneath. Her blunt teeth nibble at my lower lip, and when she arches her back slightly, settling the heat between her thighs more fully on top of me, I nearly lose control.

A feral growl rumbles in my chest, and I don't waste any more time. I drink her in, the delicious, sweet scent of her, and I deepen the kiss, my fingers wrapped around the back of her neck as she writhes against me.

She smells more like home than anything I've ever breathed before.

Everything about her is simply *right*, a puzzle piece slotted into my life. Willow perfectly fits me.

Now I just have to convince her that I'll never leave.

I'll never want for anything as long as she's by my side.

"Tell me what you want," I growl, needing her fiercely. My hands clench around her thighs, and her lids flutter as her back arches. The motion sends her hips towards me, the heat between her legs begging to be touched.

A moment ticks by, then another, and she finally looks me

right in the eyes, nearly causing my heart to skip a beat. My cock's hard as a rock in my pants, and despite barely sleeping last night, there's only one thing I want to do in bed—and it's not rest.

"Everything," she says, her voice low and husky and purely irresistible.

I don't waste any time. My mouth finds hers as my fingers glide over the button closure on the front of her thick wool pants, working them open as her small, delicate hands grip my face. Her tongue tangles with mine, and when the tip of it brushes against my fangs, I nearly spend in my pants.

A growl rumbles through my chest and throat, and when my fingers finally find the wet heat of her core, she arches back against the chair.

My gaze devours her as avidly as my mouth desires to.

"Show me what you like," I command.

Her chest rises and falls rapidly, and she moans as her fingers join mine between her legs.

"Look how fucking perfect you are," I tell her, earning another breathy sound.

The tips of her fingers make quick, gentle circles around her clit, and I fucking love how my blushing female isn't shy about this.

When she wraps her hand around mine, making me mimic her own motions, my hips jerk as my cock releases.

"That's all it takes for me, Willow. This pretty pink cunt, so fucking wet and ready for me."

Her fingernails dig into my wrist, and I hiss my surprised approval before clutching at her thighs and spreading her further apart.

The better to taste her.

She's sweet as honey on my tongue, and the way she rakes her fingers across my scalp only drives my desire for her higher.

Despite the warmth of my spend, my cock's already hard

again, and I lap at her essence as she rides my face towards her pleasure.

"More," she moans, and I groan in approval as I thrust a finger inside her hot channel. I watch her face, her eyes heavy-lidded as she works her hips in time with my tongue. When I add a second finger, stretching her around me, she gasps.

And when I crook my fingers inside her, finding the spot and stroking it, she shatters with my name on her lips.

I don't stop, nothing could tear me away from my mate, and I lap at the proof of her pleasure until she's writhing again, working towards another orgasm.

My own need doesn't matter. Nothing matters but bringing her pleasure, nothing exists outside the two of us in this moment.

I could do this forever.

Finally, she pushes my head away, gasping for air.

A sheen of sweat sparkles on her forehead, her beautiful face more relaxed and flushed than I've ever seen it before.

"I can't come again," she starts, but gasps as I drag my fangs along her clit, her hands clenching in my hair.

I let out a low chuckle. "You can."

"I can't," she insists, pushing me away, but her soft smile tells me she very well knows that I could bring her to the edge again.

"Later?" I ask, and she gives me a shy nod that has me reaching for her, needing another kiss.

Needing her to show me she feels the same way about me as I do about her—or, at the very least, that she could.

CHAPTER 12

WILLOW

I don't quite know what to do with myself.

I don't quite know if I've ever felt this... relaxed. My whole body seems to be humming, a low buzz of limp muscles too well-pleased to be anything but relaxed and satisfied.

Not to mention, I'm so suddenly aware of every inch of my body that I don't think I could go back to the way I have been living.

Quiet. Unnoticed.

I've never felt alive like I do now, unraveled and unkempt in my kitchen chair, in the arms and lap of a silver-haired fae prince who says I'm his mate.

I know that I am tired of arguing the point.

All my well-reasoned logic about why I shouldn't be with Kieran, why I shouldn't enjoy myself, are still there, crowding the back of my mind.

"We should set some relationship rules," I blurt out, surprising both of us.

He stares at me with those otherworldly eyes, the color so intense I could get lost in them.

"Anything you want."

I pinch the bridge of my nose, then drop my hands to the waist of my pants.

Kieran's hands slide against my skin as he helps me redress. It's intimate and unexpectedly sweet, and the simple gesture makes my throat tighten.

What I want from him is so much more than pleasure.

"Tell me," he urges, his hands gripping the tops of my thighs, so large they easily span their width. "I would give you the world."

"I don't know what mating means to you." It's not what I meant to say.

It's a whole lot less loaded than saying *I want to be loved and cherished*. It will hurt a lot less if, somehow, he got his memories back and decided this was all a horrible idea.

I swallow against the guilt and raw emotions.

His palms rub against the wool fabric of my trousers, the light purple of his skin standing out in stark relief against the taupe.

"It means forever," he says, and his own throat bobs as he stares at me. As if he's overwhelmed by emotion, too.

Dare to dream.

"Forever," I repeat faintly.

He reaches out, pausing before touching me, then his palm makes contact with my cheek, his thumb stroking over my cheekbone. "It means our lives are bound together, our very souls entwined. It means what makes you happy brings me joy, what brings you pleasure makes mine, and what ails you becomes my problem to find a solution to. It means I cannot bear to think of living without you, that the very thought of it brings me a pain so sharp it feels like heartbreak."

"Oh." The syllable whuffs out of me in surprise.

"Oh, indeed," he agrees, a sly smile on his face as he traces a thumb over my lips.

"Where will we live?"

"Wherever you want."

"What if you are invited back to the Underhill?"

"There is nothing for me there," he says, not even pausing long enough to consider it, not even breaking eye contact. "My life is with you. You are my home. Where you go, I follow."

I clear my throat, overwhelmed, and lean back against the chair. It creaks, and I make a mental note to check the bolts. Like everything else in this house, I'm sure the kitchen table and chairs could use some work.

I could use some, too, because what Kieran is offering sounds too good to be true.

"What if you remember you hate me?"

The determination in his eyes softens, turning molten and hot. Heavy.

"Then I'll also remember this moment, when you looked like you might cry at the thought, and despise myself for ever letting you believe such a blatant untruth."

I sniffle, because he's right. I feel like I might cry, straddling the ledge between wanting him and fear, between hope for the future and uncertainty at what it holds.

"What if you do—"

"Enough," he says, the word crisply but gently delivered. "You are my mate. What passed between us before has no bearing on how I feel for you now, and nothing can change that."

"But—"

"Nothing."

We both startle as the sound of claws on wood interrupts us. Something's scratching at the door, and whatever it is, it sounds large.

A shiver of dread goes down my spine.

When a mournful howl goes up, though, and Chirp wings silently from the room, I relax.

"It's Nerissa's wolf familiar," I tell Kieran.

"Great timing," he says drily, raising an eyebrow. "So much for your rules."

I snort in amusement, but make myself get up and go to the front door.

Sure enough, the wolf is out front, holding a rolled parchment in between delicate teeth. Chirp glides through the front door, slowing to perch on a large juniper at the edge of the forest, watching the wolf with wide, cautious eyes.

I hold my hand out and the wolf deposits the letter in my palm before turning and loping back into town.

"The coven is holding an emergency meeting," I say, unsurprised but unsettled all the same. "They want to meet at The Listening Page."

"I'm coming with you," he says, his hand on the small of my back.

Not a moment later, he's wrapped my thickest coat around my shoulders, a soft, fuzzy scarf wound around my neck.

"What about you?" I ask him. "Won't you be cold?"

"I'm fae," he says, as if that answers everything.

I tilt my head.

"It's cold in the Underhill." His lips purse slightly, and I wonder if he's remembering more than just that. I don't know if I even want to pry.

"All right," I say, closing the heavy arched door behind me and locking it with the key I keep at my waist. "We can find you a coat while we're out. I would hate for your wings to get frostbite."

His wings ruffle in response, the vibration soothing as he places my hand in the crook of his elbow. Chirp wastes no time in joining us, lighting upon the leather patch on my shoulder I sewed in for that very purpose.

"So, rules," Kieran says, steering me towards where the

cobblestone path that leads into town begins. My greenhouse and shop are too large to fit in the town proper, and while the trek into town can be obnoxious, usually I enjoy the solitude of the walk.

Kieran's company is welcome now, though, and my cheeks pink. My muscles all clench reflexively, in memory of the pleasure he's just wrung from my body.

"Right," I say, the word a bit more flimsy and weak than I anticipated. "I think we should take it slow."

His hand covers mine, warm and strong and possessive enough that a shiver goes down my spine, one that has nothing to do with the cold.

"It, as in...?" he asks, and I blink, glancing up at him.

His forehead's smooth, no sign of sarcasm on his handsome face.

"Er," I manage. I'm not sure there's any putting what we want physically from each other back in the bag. "As in the whole, ah, mated thing. The forever thing."

"Well," he draws out the word, the corners of his eyes crinkling in amusement.

I drag my attention away from him, studying the frosted cobblestones underfoot instead. Much less attractive than the fae at my side. At my arm.

"The thing about forever is that we have a long time to go at whatever speed you wish." There is a touch of irony in his inflection, but he seems more amused at my word choice than making fun of me.

Caught between embarrassment and that intense *want* for him that I'm apparently utterly unable to shake, I glance back up at him and attempt to clarify.

"I mean, we should take our time to, you know, get to know each other?" It comes out wispy, unsure, and I swallow my apprehension and tilt my head up, irritated at myself.

Heavy clouds drape over the sky, a thick blanket of them that promises wet weather. My nose scrunches because it looks like snow—but certainly it's much too early in the season for that.

"What do you want to know about me? What will set your mind at ease?" he asks, his hand still covering mine.

The closer we get to the heart of town, the more townsfolk are bustling about. More than one casts a trepidatious look up at the sky, and the threat of snow seems more likely the longer I watch them.

The longer I avoid answering his questions.

"I want to know what kind of, ah—" I flounder for the right word, completely at a loss.

"Mate," he supplies, then surprises me by leaning down and kissing my forehead, just a swift brush of his lips against my skin.

One that sends me reeling with delight, nonetheless.

"Right," I manage. "That. What does that look like?" I smooth my free hand over my wool pants, then tuck it back in my pocket.

Kieran steers me around a centaur, his wings buzzing slightly.

"It looks like this morning. It looks like me cherishing what fate has gifted me, and never taking you for granted. It looks like a lifetime of it."

I glance up at him, waiting for the punchline, waiting for him to pull away and tell me he's been joking this whole time.

But he's serious.

"I will go as slow as you want. If that means keeping a distance from you, though…" He trails off as we pass by a female minotaur and her young calf, who stares at Kieran as if he's never seen the fae before. Maybe he hasn't.

I've kept him fairly busy at my shop.

"You need to like it here," I pronounce firmly. "This is my home."

"I do like it here."

"But do you even remember any alternatives?" I know the answer to that, and I'm not sure why I'm still trying to talk us both out of the inevitable.

Probably because I've never been great at giving up control, and even though I want Kieran, have desperately wanted him, I don't like feeling that I've suddenly been paired up with him through none of our own will.

"Does it bother you? That fate's just... lumped us together? That you don't have memory of your past or a say in the future?" I whisper the questions furiously, feeling wronged on his behalf.

"Not at all." The words are final. "I have you. A mate. I am free from whatever it is that held me back from you in the first place. If my future is with you, then that is no doubt a brighter future than anything in my past, whether I remember it or not."

We've stopped, and my gaze darts between his eyes, but there's no hint of anything but the strongest conviction I've seen from him.

"Why is it you still don't trust me?"

The question shatters the fragile wall I've tried to construct between us, all my defenses laid bare.

I could lie in this moment.

I could try to rebuild my resolve, brick by brick.

I'm so, so tired of being strong, though.

Instead, I sniffle and lean my forehead against his chest. His arm goes around my back, warm even through my thick coat, and I breathe in the scent of his skin, committing it to memory.

"I am afraid of being hurt," I finally tell him. "I am afraid that you'll wake up one day and remember why you... why you behaved so coldly towards me, and that this will be the dream that breaks me completely."

The words choke out of me, true and muffled against his skin.

"If I could go back in time and change however abominably it is that I behaved towards you, I would, sweet Willow witch." He sighs, his chest rising and falling against my cheek, clinging to him like a spider mite on a glossy green leaf. "All I can do, however, is show you that I mean what I say, and that, my darling, I promise to do with every breath I take. All I want from you is… you."

"Not much to ask," I say softly, and he chuckles, the sound nearly lost in the growing hubbub of the lively downtown.

"It is everything," he says. "You have bespelled me, and for that, I am eternally gratefully."

I blink, something about his words catching in my brain, unsticking something I didn't know was even stuck.

"Willow, Kieran!" a voice calls out, and I jerk away from his embrace like a child caught with contraband sweets. "There you are, come on!"

It's Wren, Caelan stalking beside her. A medium-sized dog bounds next to the other fae's long legs, and I tilt my head at it in surprise.

No matter how often I see the creature, it surprises me that he's no longer old and decrepit, but a young, still-growing and lovely-looking dog.

"Heel, Boner," Caelan scolds, and I bite my lip to keep from laughing.

A lovely dog with a truly unfortunate name.

Wren catches my eye and rolls hers. Fenn, her red fox familiar, races along the street, nose twitching as he sniffs furiously at the air.

"We're not done discussing this," Kieran tells me in a low voice, his eyes serious but warm. "You haven't set any rules yet, and I fully expect you to tell me exactly what you need and want from me, darling Willow."

Darling Willow.

I can't quite keep from smiling up at him at the new title.

"Okay," I say, feeling lighter just for having said my piece.

Maybe I should try communicating openly more often.

Who could say?

"Hurry up, it's freezing," Caelan gripes, holding the door open for the two of us.

As if it's heard, a frigid wind gusts through the streets, blowing my hair around my face and sending The Listening Page's wood-carved sign creaking as it swings overhead.

I frown.

The wind, even in Wild Oak Woods, cannot hear.

Can it?

CHAPTER 13

WILLOW

Ruby's bookstore smells nearly as much like home as my own greenhouse and shop.

Something about the scent of paper and ink and many, many books will always feel like home, and I pause as the door closes behind me, breathing it in, soaking it in.

Kieran's hand is at the small of my back, but he doesn't push me ahead or tug at me in any way.

He's simply there, a comforting presence, and one I'm suddenly intensely grateful for.

"We'll get your memories back," I tell him, tilting my face up to him.

"As you wish," he responds, and glee rushes through me as he brushes his mouth against mine, a sweet, gentle gesture that's just as delicious as everything he did to me in my kitchen only a short while ago.

"Oh, look at you two," Piper coos, looking totally thrilled. Velvet, her deer familiar, is curled up by the stone hearth, where a fire roars in the grate. Comfortable chairs are arranged in a circle, and as far as coven meeting places go, The Listening Page is my favorite.

Especially since Piper still manages to provide refreshments.

Ga'Rek's busy setting out trays of sandwiches and cookies, and there's a large steaming pitcher of tea on an enchanted warmer on the low table centered between the chairs.

"Is it a coven meeting if non-witches attend?" Nerissa asks archly, tossing her black hair behind a shoulder as she glowers at all of us.

I grin at her, though, and she winks at me, eyeing Kieran's touch on my lower back.

"We want to help," Kieran tells her, matching her imperious tone.

Violet clears her throat, looking distinctly uncomfortable with the tension. "I think anyone who wants to be here should be here." Her voice is firm, despite the uncertainty on her face.

"I agree," Wren says, and Piper nods as they both look at me.

In fact, everyone is now looking at me. At me, and at Kieran, who wraps his arm fully around my waist. I don't think I like the attention as much as I imagined I might.

Chirp rocks slightly on his perch on my coat before taking off and settling high on a wreath above the fireplace mantel.

No one's ever looked to me as the deciding vote before. Not that I can remember, and if so, never on something as important as this.

Which is the crux of the question, really.

"Of course they should stay," I answer decisively, surprising myself. "They live here. What happens next impacts us all."

"So you think the rest of the villagers should have a say?" Ruby asks, wringing her hands. "We could call a town meeting—"

"No," Piper answers, echoing my own thoughts. "We might be well-liked here, but we all know too well what could happen if witchcraft is to blame for our current predicament. We handle this as a coven, since we shoulder the burden."

"Wild magic doesn't differentiate between magic users and regular folk," Nerissa adds drily. "The burden will be everyone's."

"So you think we should invite the whole town?" I ask her, flummoxed.

"No." She snorts in derision. "They're just as likely to pick two of us and throw us into the woods for the gods with pitchforks."

"You don't believe that," Ruby tells her testily.

Violet hugs herself, her face pale.

"You're scaring her," I admonish Nerissa.

"They might, though," Nerissa says glumly, picking at a dried speck on her leather pants.

"It's what they did to me." Violet's voice is pitched so low I almost miss it, but the room falls silent at her quiet words as if she shouted them.

"We won't let that happen," Ruby says crisply, standing up straighter.

"Neither will they," Violet says.

At that, I startle.

"They?" I ask.

Kieran's fingers dig into my waist.

"You are communicating with them, aren't you?" Piper's voice is hushed, and Ga'Rek pulls her against his chest.

Caelan, who's been unusually somber, watches her carefully, Wren at arm's length in the chair beside his.

Violet's throat bobs. "The wild magic isn't their magic. They want to protect us." Her voice is all but a hushed whisper. "They're bound to this place." Her eyes take on a far-off look, staring at something none of us can see.

The hair prickles on the back of my neck, and I press into Kieran's side.

I've seen plenty of magic in my life, so much that it's commonplace, ordinary.

What Violet is doing is anything but ordinary.

Not inviting the rest of the town in to witness her magic is the right move, there's no doubt in my mind. If I'm unsettled by it… the many species that make their home here will be, too. And that?

That never leads to happy outcomes for witches.

No, better to keep this behind closed doors.

"The spell you did on me. The summoning spell and binding…" Caelan pauses, bending down to scratch his dog's chest. Fenn watches from his spot on Wren's lap.

"We could try it," Wren muses, raising an eyebrow at Nerissa.

"Something with the power of an elder creature is not the same as some Unseelie trickster," Nerissa announces, waving her hand dismissively.

"That's quite rude," Caelan drawls.

"If I recall correctly, that ended up with more than either of you bargained for," I say plainly.

Kieran snorts, and Caelan glares at him. "As if whatever spell you're under is any better," he mutters.

At that, Kieran releases me from his grasp, thrusting his sleeve up. The tattoo stands out in stark relief against his lilac skin.

Caelan, however, looks bored. "No surprise there. Congratulations on your mating."

Ga'Rek whoops, pulling Kieran away from me and into a huge hug. "I'm pleased for you. May you both find immense happiness."

Wren and Piper are both beaming at me, and though my heart feels warm and full, I can't help the thread of guilt.

"No wonder the Elder Gods want to make brides of us," Nerissa says darkly. She cocks her head at us. "You all are disgustingly in love."

"I think it's sweet," Rosalina interjects for the first time, smiling warmly at us.

I don't say anything, though, making myself smile back at them in spite of the guilt weighing on me. Kieran can't remember who he is—how could he possibly love me? Anything he feels is a result of his mate bond, nothing more.

My stomach sinks at the truth of that thought.

I'm so suddenly miserable.

"They don't want to be summoned." Violet's voice is miniscule, her gaze on the floor. "And they can't be bound."

The atmosphere turns tense, full of crackling energy that sends me back into Kieran's arms, seeking safety there despite all my strange, jumbled up feelings.

"How do you know?" Ruby whispers the questions, the fire loud in the grate. Her cat yowls from near the front door, and when Violet raises her head, the blood drains from my face.

Her eyes are full white.

"They're already here."

CHAPTER 14

WILLOW

"Don't move from my side," Kieran mutters in my ear, and I nod, though I doubt my feet could take me an inch from him.

A book on the table opens, the pages whipping on an unseen wind.

The pressure in the bookstore builds, like the moments before a storm breaks, and I suck in a breath as the temperature drops.

"They're here," Violet says again, and this time, her eyes are back to their normal, human shade.

My mouth is dry with fear.

Kieran's wings vibrate behind him as he tucks me further into his body.

"They won't take you. You're mine. We belong to each other."

Two forms materialize in front of the hearth, and Velvet the deer scurries behind the safety of Piper and Ga'Rek.

Max, Ruby's cat familiar, hisses as the shapes become more solid, taking form as the fire casts long, haunting shadows all around them.

"Only two," I say on an exhale. Of course. The third took the poor duchess.

"Two is enough," Kieran says roughly.

He's so protective, his hands possessive and hot on me, and I should resist it, but I like it too much to pull away.

I like the idea of being his too much.

I like him most of all.

Slowly, the shadows congeal, and two forms of ancient magic stand before our coven, in Ruby's bookstore.

"Odd place for two gods to show up," Nerissa says in a low voice. "Thought you two might feel more at home in the ancient myths section instead of where our romance book club meets."

Both males turn to her, and something like a smile shifts across the vicious features of the horned one. His antlers nearly scrape the ceiling, lichen-covered and ancient. His eyes are the most vivid green I've ever seen outside a plant, and Nerissa's wolf growls low in his throat as he contemplates my coven sister.

"We wish no harm on Wild Oak Woods."

"Our new sister sent advice," the other elder being intones, his face shifting from skeletal in one second to normal, if otherworldly handsome, in the next.

"You mean the duchess," Violet says, and there's fire under the phrase.

He inclines his head, a hint of a smile playing along his face. "Just so."

The fire pops, and I jump at the sound.

"The duchess, the bride of our brother, tells us that our methods are…" He clears his throat, mostly male-looking now, though something preternatural and dark looks out of his eyes. "Outdated."

"I think her exact words were brutish, boorish, and barbaric," the horned god adds, looking…

I squint, trying to paw past Kieran's iron grip on me to get a better look.

He looks... amused. He lifts an eyebrow, staring down the huge wolf at Nerissa's side. "The alliteration was also hers."

"She's not wrong," Wren says.

"I think it's stylish," Caelan says slyly. "Demanding a bride from a coven of powerful women in return for protection of their beloved town? It's a classic. How can you improve on it?"

No one answers. Wren buries her face in her hands, and I'm not sure if she's laughing or disappointed in Caelan.

"Boner says there is no room for improvement." The dog perks up at his name. "What Boner says is truth—"

A huge sigh escapes the horned god. "Enough, trickster."

The other god sets a hand on his brother's shoulder. "We cannot be bound, or summoned, not as you were. We are elementals, and we wish no harm or suffering upon any of you, but for our magic to work, we must abide by the rules, which means we must take brides from your coven." His gaze slips to my face, and Kieran snarls—snarls!—at his interest.

I tuck myself more firmly against him.

"It seems as though one more of you has been claimed," he muses.

"We do not have time to court you as you and our new sister deserve," the horned god continues, finally tearing his eyes away from Nerissa. "But we all prefer our witches willing. We have come to tell you we will be a part of your town now. So that it will be no hardship for those of you who are in want of a powerful male to find us on your own."

No one speaks, or moves, and I hardly dare breathe.

"What if we don't—" Nerissa starts, but the horned god holds up a hand, crusted with several bone-and-wood rings.

"You will. The right ones will be drawn to us. Our magic is as wild as that which threatens, and like calls to like." He dips his head, his antlers threatening to scrape the iron candelabra hanging from the ceiling. "You will see more of us soon, witches."

They disappear slowly, fading into nothingness.

The silence they leave in their wake lasts a long moment—and then everyone's talking at once.

CHAPTER 15

KIERAN

Mine.

They recognize Willow as mine, as they very well should.

Triumph floods me, only stopped short by the fact my witch is still tense and trembling with anxiety.

For her friends. For her town.

Guilt dulls my sense of victory and I tuck her closer to me, burying my nose in her rosemary-and-mint-scented hair. "We will help your friends."

"They don't need help, they need a clever seamstress," Caelan announces, and I realize I spoke too loudly.

Everyone stares at Caelan, even his dog, who's still warming himself by the fire.

"For their wedding garments, obviously," he flicks a hand through the air, and a growl of dismay rattles in my chest.

"If they do not wish to wed, then we will not force them. I will not be part of having any of their free will taken away."

"It's just two—" Caelan starts.

"Enough," Wren tells him, her eyes narrowing to furious slits. "These are my friends you're talking about—"

"You and Willow and Piper seem happy enough. I haven't given you any reason to complain." He clicks his tongue and shakes his head. "How do you know these elemental creatures will be any different? They're moving to town, aren't they? None of you have to, you know, be abducted against your will and moved to what I'm sure are palatial, magical residences—"

"That's not the point," Nerissa snaps, looking fiery and wild.

Much too harsh for my tastes, that one. No, I prefer my soft and lovely Willow… to everything, perhaps.

"The point is that none of us want to be forced into what appears to be an eternal bond," Nerissa finishes, and her wolf familiar sits up on massive paws and stares, unblinking, at her.

"I'll do it," Violet says, her voice quiet but strong. Determined. "I don't have a place here, not like the rest of you." The words rush out of her, into the stunned silence she's created.

"Violet—" Nerissa starts, but Violet holds up her hand.

Willow's face pales. "You don't need to do that—"

"Absolutely not—"

"Why would you want to—"

The witches explode at once, then pause to glance around at each other.

Ruby stands, pacing the length of the hearth, which means she has to step over the deer lying in the way as Boner tracks her progress with sad hound eyes.

Willow's lips are pressed in a thin line, and Piper looks ready to pounce if anyone else so much as utters that they're considering the offer of marriage.

"Why shouldn't I?" Violet asks, and there's a hint of stubbornness under her sweet-natured tone that surprises me.

It shouldn't surprise me, considering each woman in this room is about as tractable as a decades-old fruitcake. You're more likely to break your tooth arguing with one than to get anywhere with an entire coven of them.

"Why are you set on it?" I counter, as gently as possible.

Willow nods fervently, still tucked in so tight to me that her head rubs against my chest. Piper throws me a grateful look, and Wren's shoulders relax slightly.

"Because I have nothing to lose. No one to lose. No business to keep, no magic I know of, and—" Her voice falters and she goes silent, looking to the shadows dancing in the back of the fireplace.

We're silent, waiting for her to finish.

"You're drawn to him." Nerissa's voice is weary, and when I glance back at her, she's rubbing her temple. Her hand dips down to a locket on a long chain around her neck, and her fingers smooth across the surface.

Violet doesn't answer, but the determined set to her eyes says everything she doesn't voice.

"Right, then. Well. Perhaps we'll get more answers when the duchess returns to town. With them." Ruby pauses her pacing, her hands on her hips. "I've been researching wild magic," she continues. "Having ancient elemental powers like the ones these… er, suitors are offering does appear to be the most likely way of controlling the impact."

"Suitors?" Caelan drawls.

Wren smacks his arm, and he laughs.

Ruby glares at him, power crackling along her skin.

Caelan raises his eyebrows before dropping his gaze to his dog. "Suitors it is."

I stifle a laugh because this will go down in memory as one of the few times Caelan has been silenced by a mere look, and not one from his blonde mate.

In memory.

I stiffen, letting the conversation ebb and flow around me as it hits me all at once.

I remember Caelan.

I remember our lives in the Underhill, with the Dark Queen... my mother.

My hand falls away from Willow's gentle curves, and my breath stutters as it all comes rushing back.

I remember it all.

And I remember why Willow thought I hated her.

Because I wanted her to.

CHAPTER 16

WILLOW

Something's wrong, and not just due to the fact Violet and maybe even Nerissa are considering marrying the damned elemental Elder Gods or whatever in the seven hells they're calling themselves.

It's Kieran.

Tension threads through his shoulders and back, his wings slightly elevated, but for once, not even so much as vibrating.

The coven meeting devolves around us, with Ruby lecturing Violet as Nerissa argues with Piper and Wren. Rosalina chimes in as needed, and Boner the dog stands erect on his hindlegs and lets out a piteous wail.

"What is it?" I ask him in a low voice. My heart races beneath my breast, and I don't need him to answer as my stomach drops.

Does he remember?

His once warm gaze is iced over, cold enough to make me quail.

Maybe it's me; maybe he's realized, with all this talk of marriage and mates, that he doesn't want me after all. Especially with all the other witches in this room, so much more powerful and exciting than I am.

"I'm hungry," he says, smiling down at me. "It surprised me."

I squint up at him, confused. The ice I thought I saw is gone—his smile real and just as thrilling as ever. His hand goes to the small of my back, and then he wraps his arms around me, leaning down.

"Even if you weren't mine, even if you weren't my mate—I could never let you go."

His words thaw me the rest of the way and I return the hug, hungry for his touch. A quick glance around tells me everyone is still arguing about what to do, and I certainly don't have anything to add to the current conversation.

"Come on," I tell him, tugging him behind me through The Listening Page Bookstore. "Let's go get some food and supplies before that winter storm that's brewing hits." I can't quite bring myself to look back at him.

I'm not sure I can meet his eyes—I'm afraid of what I'll see there. Regret. Disdain.

The ice that finally melted when he lost his memories.

Guilt gnaws at me, a hungry rat I can't seem to cage. I shove it down, uneasy, and the bell above the door to The Listening Page tinkles as I push it open.

"Where are you two going?" Piper calls out.

"I need supplies." The words come out sharp enough to cut, and I inhale through my nose, pausing in the doorway. Cold air rushes in, laced with the metallic scent of snow. "Storm is coming."

I try to gentle my voice and turn over one shoulder, offering an apologetic look.

"You are a part of this coven," Wren says, and Nerissa nods her agreement.

"You should have a say in our decisions." Nerissa flicks her dark fall of hair over one shoulder.

Wind whips through the open door, and the fire gutters in the hearth.

"This isn't a decision that can be made by a group of people, coven or not, magical or not." I nod, then exhale, my eyes fluttering shut. "I don't know of any magic that could be helpful at all—and if the two of you wish to wed them, then that's not something I'm willing to change anyone's minds on. If you have a plan that requires plant magic to thwart them, then let me know. Otherwise, I need things in town before this storm hits."

Hurt and shock marks the faces of my friends, and I turn around quickly so I don't have to see it.

It's not independence or any sort of moral high ground that has me nearly running through the door.

No, it's sheer cowardice, because if I have to spend another hour in their company while they debate what to do and Kieran might be remembering why he despises me... I think I might just fall apart.

CHAPTER 17

WILLOW

"Thank the goddess this is a small town," I murmur, walking as quickly as I dare on the already slick cobblestones. Sleet began falling as soon as we left Ruby's bookstore, and it didn't take long for the fits and starts and icy drizzle to give way to frigid rain in earnest.

"I could walk you home and shop for you if you make me a list, my love," Kieran says, managing to keep me upright as I lose my footing on an especially icy patch.

His wings vibrate dully, shedding a fresh layer of ice.

Despite the temperature drop, his words warm me from the inside out.

His love.

"Do you mean that?" I ask, pausing under the awning at my favorite green grocer's stand.

"Of course, I would be happy to take care of you in every way." He lifts one eyebrow, a slow smirk raising the corners of his mouth.

I laugh in spite of myself and all my misgivings at his blatant innuendo, but it quickly dies on my lips.

"That's not what you were asking, was it?" He pulls me in close and I let myself lean against him, soaking up both his warmth and his touch.

I nod when the silence grows longer between us.

"I called you that because it's true. I'm sorry if it upset you or caught you off guard—"

Pulling back, I press my finger to his lips. "I just wanted to know if you meant it."

He grins at me, then kisses the pad of my index finger. "I meant it, Willow."

The centaur, Marie, coughs delicately to get our attention, and we turn to her together, fresh heat rising on my cheeks.

"What can I do for you, Willow? I'm packing up and heading out, trying to get home before this weather turns any worse." Marie's hooves clop on the cobbles as she adjusts the apron string around her neck.

"Kale, potatoes, any fresh vegetables you have left," I tell her.

"Mushrooms," Kieran adds.

"Mushrooms," I agree.

I mostly grow my own berries and some produce for myself, but with Kieran living with me, I'll need a few extra things.

Living with me. My breath catches in my chest as the centaur packs up a wooden crate for me and Kieran leans down, pressing his lips against the skin on my neck.

His love. His mate.

It still seems too good to be true, and I can't shake the niggling feeling that something is very, very wrong, that he's going to remember why he didn't like me in the first place.

It will shatter me when he leaves.

But... at least, maybe, for now, I can just live in this moment.

"I wouldn't mind trading you for some of your raspberries and other summer produce, you know. My offer stands."

"I know, and I wish I had a big enough space to grow enough for you. Most of my energy goes towards the medicinal and—"

"And craft herbs, I know," the centaur finishes for me, smiling down at me. "I put some edible flowers in there; they'll make a nice salad. We had extra arugula as well, so that's in there for you too."

It takes only a moment longer to pay, and we thank her before continuing on.

"What else do you need?"

I pause at the window of the Elven Wish Boutique, a bespoke atelier that I'm not quite sure how it manages to stay in business in our small town. Perhaps, like Wren, the owner has a lot of merchandise she ships out.

For whatever reason, she made Wild Oak Woods her home, too. I've hardly seen her, both of us too busy at our respective stores, but her shiny platinum hair isn't what's caught my eye in the window now.

No, it's the lovely teal silk dress that has me stopped and staring in the persistent sleet. Teal-green silk skims the figure of a mannequin, hugging tight around the waist before falling away at the hips. A slit climbs from the bottom of the skirt to a truly high place at the thigh. Off-the-shoulder diaphanous sleeves billow around the cleverly sculpted arms.

"Do you like that?" Kieran asks. "I would enjoy peeling that off your perfect body." His fingers grip my hip, and I force out an embarrassed laugh.

"Come on," I tell him, forcing my feet to walk again. "I want some of Lila's tea, and her shop is quite a bit further, plus we still need some meat from the butcher. And cheese, if they're not out."

Despite the awful weather, the downtown area is still clogged with people and creatures, all doing the same thing we are—stocking up before the storm.

Although, perhaps, we're all a little late, because it's clear the storm is very much upon us now.

Wind whips my red curls around my face, the cold air stinging my skin and eyes as we do our best to finish the errands we need to run before the storm hits. By the time we make it to Lila's Long Leaf Brews, the tip of my nose feels frozen and my breath crystalizes in front of my face.

I adjust the packages in my arms, attempting to reach for the door handle when it opens from within.

"Hello, Willow, Kieran. You've barely made it in time; we were just about to close up shop and hunker down." Druze, Lila's husband and new business partner, ushers us inside with a broad smile.

He's the only male dryad I've ever seen, and even though he's lived here for months now, his greenish tinted skin and huge frame still take me a moment to adjust to. There's something different and otherworldly about him compared to Ga'Rek, too, who I've been around a lot more and have grown completely accustomed to. I scooch inside past him, nearly fumbling the wax paper and twine wrapped meat, but Kieran manages to catch me and our groceries up in his arms before I ruin them.

"Thank you," I say on an exhale.

"Don't thank me," he says, a bit curtly, and I blink in surprise before he smiles down at me again, chasing some of the worry away. "You deserve someone who will always catch you."

"Willow!" Lila calls from the back storeroom, appearing in the doorway. "And Kieran. What a nice surprise."

I inhale deeply, savoring the incredible herbal aroma of her shop. I am fully capable of making my own tea, as is every witch, but Lila's elven knack for herbs and flavors will always put my sad attempts to shame. Her tea is worth every single cent.

"I love this place," I tell her honestly, my eyes devouring the interior as if they've been starved for stimulation. There are several dozen tables, all done with different creatures' and species' preferences in mind. Two rooms branch off the main one, and those are decorated thematically, too.

The whole space is magical, and a good reminder that not all magic comes from witchery—some people are simply gifted.

"And I love that you love it. Having Wild Oak Woods' best apothecary and green witch love my work is about as big a compliment as I could ever imagine." Lila takes the packages from my hands, setting them down on an empty table before drawing me into her arms for a hug. "It's been a while."

"You're mated," Druze says, the shock in his voice startling me out of Lila's arms.

Is he upset? Does he think we're a bad match? He must know how much Kieran despised me, or that he has amnesia—

"I'm so happy for you, Kieran," Druze explodes, beaming as he drags my prince into a hug of his own, thumping him heartily on the back.

Lila crows, hugging me again as she hops from foot to foot. She claps her hands in glee as she pulls away to study us both.

"We have to celebrate," she says, her joy shining on her face.

"We, uh, ah, we have to get home before the storm—"

"Not right now, you goose, but soon. Oh, we can have a party here, don't you think, Druze?" She spreads her hands wide, encompassing the whole space. "Candlelit, dinner in six courses, tea paired with each, don't you think?"

"Lila, you don't have to do that—"

"I want to," she enthuses, taking my hands in hers. "It's what you deserve." She reaches for Kieran, tucking him into her side, where he towers over her slender frame. "Both of you. Oh, I'm just so happy right now."

"If it helps, she's been wanting to throw more parties here. Extend the business," Druze explains, his green eyes twinkling in the tea shop's low light. "You'll give her an excuse and an example to expand."

"Oh."

"We don't have to if you don't want to, or we could do something just a little small, you know, elegant and simple." Lila wrings her hands, eyes searching mine.

"Willow is still adjusting to our new status," Kieran tells her, not unkindly, but it makes me feel uncomfortable and ungrateful all at once.

"I just need to think about it. It's not a no." My voice sounds small to my own ears.

"Of course, of course, I'm sorry, I should have waited, that was insensitive of me to pounce all over you." Lila's clearly crestfallen, and Druze wedges between her and Kieran to wrap a muscled arm around her shoulders.

"No, not at all. It's kind and generous of you. I just need to, ah, think about it?"

Wind whips around the tea shop, howling as it tears down the street, and we all fall silent as it screams.

"We should get the tea we need and get home," Kieran says and I nod, suddenly trepidatious about braving the outdoors and that wind again.

"Tell me what you want and Druze can take the cart and horse to your house, Willow. It's too far to walk in this."

With the storm ratcheting up outside, we don't waste any time. Chirp flies off ahead of us, and I watch him disappear with a bit of worry.

I don't want my owl hurt in this storm.

Before long, though, Druze has all our packages neatly tucked in the cart, along with several tins of Lila's amazing tea. She tucks two thick wool blankets around our shoulders and legs before hopping off the cart.

"Be safe, stay warm!" she shouts over the storm, and Druze urges the horse forward at a quick trot.

It's too loud and uncomfortable to make conversation, so I huddle into Kieran's heat, his strong hand rubbing over the arm of my coat as the cart jostles along the cobblestones. The rest of the people we saw earlier are gone now, and the streets of Wild

Oak Woods are all but empty as an even darker blanket of clouds bears down on the town.

Lightning forks across the sky, illuminating the multicolored roofs. Most awnings and signage has been taken down by savvy shopkeeps, but the few left outside flap and creak in the onslaught.

"It doesn't feel natural," I mutter, eyeing the bank of clouds. The skin on the back of my neck prickles, and Druze shoots me a look of agreement before returning his attention to the draft horse.

Maybe I should look into getting a cart and horse. I wonder if Rosalina could help me source one. It would certainly make getting around town easier. Maybe with Kieran's help, we could set up a small stand on the other side of town, or do deliveries when our customers are ill.

I cut the line of thought off, shaking my head.

I won't include Kieran in any plans for the future.

My stomach turns leaden.

Not until he regains his memories and decides what it is he truly wants, mated or not.

I swallow around the thickness in my throat, the cold air like knives as I breathe.

The wind catches my scarf, blowing it from around my neck, and I yelp in surprise. Kieran, however, simply reaches over and rewinds it around my neck, his fingers making quick work of a sturdier knot and tucking it neatly within the collar of my coat.

I smile up at him, grateful, and while he returns it, he looks away quicker than I would like.

My heart drops.

Druze tugs gently on the lines and the huge horse comes to a slow stop at my front door. I take a beat, trying to collect my thoughts as Kieran easily swings down and collects the myriad of packages. I glance up at the clouds overhead, the sleet that's been icing the streets and roofs turning slowly to soft, down-feather snow.

Thunder rolls overhead, and Druze shoots me a concerned look. "You all right? It's early for a winter storm like this."

"I'm fine. Just... tired." It's a lackluster explanation, but it's not untrue. Not really. "Worried about this storm, too." I fold up the wool blanket over my legs next to him, and he nods, eyes still narrowed as he inspects me.

"If you need help, send that owl of yours, you hear? The cold doesn't bother me as much as some species. I need more sleep in the winter, but I can make it out here to help if need be."

Chirp hoots softly from my shoulder before gliding through the front door behind Kieran.

"Thank you, Druze," I tell him with a smile. "We'll be okay."

"It's not him I'm worried about," Druze replies, his expression utterly serious.

I inhale sharply, forcing the smile onto my face. "I'm fine. Kieran and I... it's new, but it's good."

I think. I'm pretty sure.

Still, misgivings and doubt crowd my thoughts as the sound of hooves and cart fade away.

"It's early still," Kieran calls from the kitchen. "I can start a stew for dinner, I think I saw a recipe for one earlier. How about a simple lunch? Cheese, some fruit? Bread?"

"You don't have to put everything away, I can do that." My cold fingers struggle with the fastenings on my coat for a long moment, and I'm on the cusp of cursing them open when warm hands find the clasps and do it for me.

"I know you can do it, but that's not the point, Willow." Kieran's voice is pitched low, gentle as a caress. "The point is I want to do it for you. I want to help you; I want to be a part of your life."

"You're here, doesn't that mean you're a part of my life?" I ask, hating how petulant the question seems, wishing I hadn't asked it… and now hanging on tenterhooks waiting for his reply.

He laughs, helping me shrug out of the coat before fixing me with a serious expression. "I want to do things for you—make your life easier. Make it a life that I'm a part of—be the mate you deserve."

I drop my gaze and take the coat from his hands, hanging it in the small closet by the door.

"What's wrong?" he asks, his hands running over my shoulders.

"I'm just tired," I make myself say.

"All the more reason to let me help you," he says, and this time, my smile is real.

"A simple lunch sounds delicious." I fix him with a stern look. "But I can help you make dinner. No ifs, ands, or buts about it."

"As if I could resist having you next to me this afternoon," he says, eyes crinkling at the corners.

"Then I need to do some work in the greenhouse and make some more elixirs."

"Good, that fits with my plans nicely," Kieran agrees, wrapping an arm around my waist as we walk to the kitchen.

"Oh, does it, now?" I ask, amused and in a better mood already. "How's that?"

"If you're tired from work tonight, you'll be much more amenable to me helping you unwind."

I make a strangled noise of surprise and pleasure. "Oh?"

"Mmhmm. I have just the thing in mind."

He pauses, a predatory grin on his face.

My core heats, and I can't help the surge of pure desire. I need him. I need him to want me like this, I need him to want me at my absolute worst.

I need him to want me no matter what.

I need him to never look at me again with that cold indifference now that I've known the heat of his heart, of his body.

"A massage, a hot bath, and warm sheets on the bed."

I laugh in spite of myself as he preens. "Oh, is that right?"

"Why, whatever in the world did you have in mind?" He smirks down at me, and another laugh trickles out of me as I shake my head, miming zipping my lips.

CHAPTER 18

WILLOW

I can't remember a more perfect day. Productive but relaxed, cozy and quiet, but with the perfect conversation partner.

Whatever weirdness I sensed from Kieran earlier in the day has evaporated, and our rapport is more natural than I can remember it being with anyone, even the other witches in my coven. He seems to sense when I need quiet to concentrate or when I need space, and makes himself useful.

And yet he's also there with a quick remark or smart observation when I'm working on the fiddlier parts of potion-making, anticipating when I needed a fresh pinch of herbs or a new wooden spoon to stir with.

I finish decanting the last of the elixirs, a pleasant ache in my shoulders as I clean out the cauldron with a spell my mother taught me when I was barely five years old.

The moment I open the door to the laboratory, the scent of the stew Kieran's been working on all afternoon hits me, making my mouth water. The sweetness of carrot, tempered with the tell-tale richness of red wine, braised beef and fresh bread.

I could definitely get used to this.

"There she is," Kieran says as I walk into the kitchen. He beams at me, lighting up from the inside in a way that makes my heart ache.

"Here I am," I agree, melting into him as he pulls me into his side.

He looks so otherworldly yet at home in my kitchen, one arm around me, the other ladling thick, fragrant stew into my bowls.

"The house doesn't need any decoration with you in it," I say out loud, earning a laugh from him. "It's true," I tell him stubbornly.

His wings reflect the light, illuminating variegated patches of greens and purples all over the walls and floor.

He brushes a kiss against my forehead. "Come on, green witch, it's time to eat. You can admire me later. I'll allow it."

A sly smile quirks up the corner of his mouth, and he sets our bowls on the table. A crusty loaf of fresh bread still steams between our plates, and he's poured two generous glasses of red wine, too. Rich yellow butter sits on one of my favorite colorful ceramic plates, and I sigh happily as I sit in the chair next to his.

"Thank you for this," I say. My throat goes tight with unexpected emotion. "For the whole day, really."

"You don't have to thank me."

"I will always thank you." I squeeze his forearm, tears threatening. "I will never take a minute of your attention and care for granted, and if I do, you have permission to remind me of how lucky I am."

His low, thick laugh reverberates around my kitchen. "Oh, and how should I remind you of that, exactly?"

Feeling slightly mischievous, I simply raise one eyebrow at him and lift my soup spoon to my mouth. It's delicious, the flavors melding to perfection, and I groan as the meat falls apart on my tongue.

Kieran groans too, but when I glance over at him, he's not

eating—no, he's watching me with a desperate look. I frown, confused... because more than anything, he looks scared.

Afraid.

A gust of wind pulls my attention to the window over the sink as the shutter outside unlatches, crashing against the wood frame.

When I look back at Kieran, he's smiling again.

I must have imagined it, or maybe he was simply reacting to the storm outside.

"I don't remember a winter storm this early—not one like this, anyway."

"We didn't have storms in the Underhill," he says casually.

The casual comment triggers a strange feeling in the back of my mind, like it's important somehow, but the shutter crashes against the window again, and my attention scatters again.

"It must be the magic of the Elder Gods, or, ah, elementals? Whatever they call themselves, I think this must be part of what they're saying they protect against."

"Or it's just an early storm," I say, spooning more of the incredible soup into my mouth. "This is so good."

"I followed the recipe, but I added a few more herbs to it. I also felt like it needed more of that tomato paste you have jarred, so I put in another half."

"It worked perfectly." I bite my lip, watching the shutter flap outside. "I should go secure that. I don't want the window to break. That would be a pain to clean up."

"I'll do it," Kieran says, standing abruptly, all but sprinting across the kitchen.

"Wait," I cry out, but he's already rounded the corner. "I didn't mean right now."

The words fall on an empty kitchen, and I can't quite shake the sense that something is different about Kieran.

Maybe it's the storm.

I mull it over, trying to put my finger on what it is, exactly, that's bothering me. The soup is the perfect accompaniment to my deep thoughts, as is the bread, and I've finished the bowl and a quarter of the loaf.

Kieran pops up off and on through the window, securing the shutter outside.

His weirdness and discomfort must be because of the storm… though he didn't hesitate to brave the heavy snow drifting down to fix the damned shutter.

I mean, he did say that he had never experienced a storm like this before.

He didn't have storms in the Underhill.

I blanch, feeling the color drain from my face. My spoon clatters into the bowl, my stomach turning as the truth hits me.

He remembers. Whatever it was that caused his amnesia… it's stopped.

My hand goes to my mouth, goosebumps rising across my arms.

The front door creaks open, wind whipping through the house, before it slams shut, Kieran's footfalls light on the floor.

"Think I got it fixed, but if this wind gets worse, there's no guarantees it will hold. We might want to board the window just in case—" his words cut off as he meets my eyes.

"You remembered," I croak. Betrayal. That's the sick, oily feeling tangling up my emotions. "Why didn't you tell me? Were you just going to pretend?"

His wings begin vibrating, a low hum that picks up speed, sending half-melted snow spattering all along the floor and walls.

A muscle in his jaw twitches in time with his wings, working overtime.

"Tell me I'm wrong," I plead, near tears. "Say something. Anything."

"I remembered," he grates out, unable to look me in the eye.

CHAPTER 19

KIERAN

"I remember," I repeat, running my hand through my hair, which only manages to send more snow and water all over the floor. "I never... I don't want to hurt you."

She doesn't respond, the devastation and hurt in her lovely eyes wounding me more deeply than any hurt distributed in my mother's toxic court.

"Well." Her chin lifts, her shoulders back. Her throat works as she exerts that iron will over herself once more, but I recognize this now for what it is—a shield. Armor of a sort, the kind that's come with being so afraid to be hurt that she's spent a lifetime crafting it.

And now I'm the reason she wears it again.

"I should have told you the minute I started to remember everything, but I..." The right words fail me.

"You should have," she agrees, and when her voice breaks on the last word, it cracks something deep inside me.

I go to my knees, needing to be near her, needing to be eye-to-eye, on even ground.

Even when the ground seems to be filled with traps I don't know how to navigate.

"I'm not perfect, Willow, and I never will be. But I am yours, and nothing I remembered will change that."

Her chin wobbles, her eyes leaking tears now.

I press my finger to one, then kiss the salty liquid from it, unwilling to waste even this from her.

"You are mine. My mate." I push the sleeve of my shirt up, so rough the button pops off the cuff in my haste. "It doesn't matter that I've remembered. The magic we have is permanent, our bond is permanent." The mate mark's still dark and strong against my skin.

The sight of it reassures me, but when I find Willow's gaze again, pain rockets through me.

Tears stream down angry red blotches on her cheeks, and the wobble in her chin has progressed to a full-on lip quiver.

"None of that, my love," I tell her, pressing my finger to her mouth. I don't understand why she's so angry. "I am yours."

"Why didn't you tell me you remembered? Is it because you hate me so much? And now you're stuck with me because of some mate magic you didn't want or ask for?"

Oh. *Oh.*

"No." I can't help the laugh of surprise and relief. I snatch her hand from her lap, pressing a kiss to her knuckles. "No. Is that what you're upset about? You think I... am stuck with you?"

"Like I'm a thorn in your side," she says miserably, sniffling. "A poisonous, toxic thorn—"

I catch her lips against mine, effectively cutting her off. The kiss deepens and she softens in my arms, before pulling away.

"Answer the question," she snaps, wrapping her arms around herself like she'll float away without them.

"I was an asshole," I tell her. "I acted abominably. Because I knew. I knew, Willow, the moment I walked into your life, that I wouldn't be walking out of it. I knew as soon as I let my guard down around you, the moment I finally kissed you, that you would be mine."

"And you hated that so much that you treated me like that—"

"Never," I tell her, not laughing this time, shaking my head. "I treated you like that, kept you at arms' length, because I will never, not in a thousand lifetimes, deserve you. I wanted more for you. I am the toxic thorn in your side, my Willow. I would be the one that dragged you down."

"You're a fae prince," she says, her jaw hanging open in surprise.

I press my palm against the side of her lovely face. "I am the unwanted spare to the Underhill throne. If my mother ever decides she wants me back or to end me once and for all, I'm a sitting duck and always have been. Being with you puts you in danger, too. You are everything that is pure and green and new in the world, the spring that's finally thawed the winter of my life."

She lets out a shaky breath, fresh tears streaming down her face.

But she leans into my hand.

Leans into my hand, and closes her eyes.

"I'm not scared of your mother."

Of all the things she might have said, that statement is the furthest from what I expected.

This time, I can't hold in my laugh, and she opens her eyes and smiles back at me weakly.

"I wanted to protect you. I wanted more for you than what an exiled ass of a fae prince could offer you. But I forgot that. I forgot all the reasons I should selflessly let you go, and now you're mine, Willow witch. I refuse to let you go." I kiss her lightly, the slightest brush of our mouths together, and the feel of her is as electric as it always is. "I refuse to be anything but selfish where you're involved."

She laughs too, though the lovely sound is broken by another shaky breath, and I pull her into my arms, just needing to hold her close, to prove to myself that she is whole and here and mine.

"You're stuck with me, Willow, not the other way around. Forgive me for wanting the fantasy of me not having a horrible past to last a bit longer. I'm sorry I hurt you, and I swear on my life that I will spend the rest of it making it up to you."

"Does it come with this bread and stew?"

"What?" I tilt my head, confused.

"Does the rest of your life making it up to me come with more of this stew and bread?"

I snort, my eyebrows lifting as high as they can physically go. "That can be arranged."

"Good." She sniffles again, then wraps herself fully around me, her arms hooked around my neck, her cheek wet against my collarbone.

When her legs wrap around my waist, I decide I'm done with dinner.

I'm ready for dessert.

CHAPTER 20

WILLOW

I am weak with relief. Weak with it.

All the fight I thought I had stored up for when this finally happened, for when Kieran finally remembered, went out my body with his simple explanation.

He wanted to protect me.

I fist the fabric of his shirt in my hands, snuggling as close as I can get to his perfect body.

"I was on the brink of giving up my foolish notion of chivalry when it came to you anyway. Spell or no spell. Amnesia just made it happen faster." He makes a chuffing noise, nuzzling my neck before inhaling deeply.

That surprises me. "What?"

"Oh, absolutely. The minute those bastards showed up and demanded a bride from your coven. I was ready to do whatever it took to make sure that you wouldn't run to one of them for the sake of your town. Selfish, like I said." He huffs a laugh, the warm air sending lightning through my spine. "You were mine, and if I had half a chance to explain how I felt to you, to apologize for being a royal thorn in the ass—"

I laugh at that, and he pulls away to smile at me.

"I looked for you that night. Then I woke up in your bed, with not a clue of anything but the knowledge that you were mine."

"I never figured out how I cast that spell." It comes out like a guilt-stained confession.

"Oh, I did. Today. When I went to the greenhouse for extra herbs."

My jaw drops. "Well, aren't you full of secrets."

"I'm fairly certain that is the last of my secrets."

"Tell me," I prod, shaking him—or trying to, but he's immovable and just laughs at my attempt.

"That flower, you know the one you were so worried about not blooming? It bloomed that night. It's been open, until today. Today, it's wilted and ready to be pruned."

"The xëchno plant," I say breathlessly. "Fascinating."

"Dangerous, really." He presses a kiss against my lips.

"The implications of a plant that casts spells without the will of a witch is… a terrifying prospect."

"Oh, it had will attached to it." He kisses the tip of my nose, each of my cheeks.

"What?"

"I wished for you. I wished you were mine." He grins against my mouth. "It was my will that made it all happen. Green magic, yes, but not yours."

My heart feels light enough to float away.

"I never stopped wishing for you either," I tell him, and it's my turn to kiss him.

His mouth slants over mine, his hand going to my hair. I want to touch him all at once. I want to run my hands across the delicious body I've been lusting over.

When we break apart, we're both short of breath. Kieran's

eyes are dilated, and when I press my hips closer to him, we both moan at the sensation.

"I have no reason not to do exactly as I please with you now," I murmur.

"I live to serve," he says seriously, and then grins when I laugh.

"Take me to bed, my mate."

It's the first time I've called him that, and for a second, my heart refuses to beat, so nervous at what he'll say to it.

I shouldn't be.

He kisses me again, thoroughly, sweetly, like it means something. Like I mean something to him.

Because it does.

Because I am.

The kiss turns fierce, and needy. My teeth scrape against his lower lip, and Kieran lets out a growl.

A *growl*.

I hardly have time to marvel at it before he's scooping me up against him, his hands tight on my ass as he strides through my house.

I can't stop kissing him, my pulse so loud in my ears it nearly drowns out his footsteps.

He stops walking, the kiss slowing, until he finally nibbles at my lip until I come up for air.

"Tell me what you—"

"I want it all," I say simply. "I want all of you."

"If you change your mind—"

"I won't." I ache for him.

How is it possible to feel any better than I already do? I have the fae of my dreams in my room.

"If you do," he says with a chuckle, setting me on the edge of my bed. "We can wait."

"I have been waiting to have my way with you since you walked into my shop." It takes me no time at all to shuck my blouse, not waiting for him to do any of the work.

I am out of patience. I want this *now*.

He sucks in a breath as my breasts are freed from the supportive undergarment, and when I glance up at him, suddenly feeling shy, he falls to his knees again.

He's making a habit of that.

"I fucking," he practically wheezes, "never seen something so beautiful as you, Willow."

His hand spans the width of the space between my shoulder blades, and then his mouth is on one nipple. His other hand works my left breast, the motions somehow expert and careful all at once.

I arch and gasp as his teeth clamp gently around the hardened peak of my breast.

"I could come from this," I babble, threading my fingers through his hair, holding on for dear life.

"Then you'll be coming all night." That same harsh predator tone is back, and I love it.

My eyes flutter shut, and I'm lost to sensation. So much sensation. His mouth pops off one breast and I nearly shriek as he blows a cold stream of air across the tip before giving my other breast the same attention.

His hand doesn't go to the one he just kissed, though_no, it trails down the soft curve of my belly, finding the buttons at my waistband.

With a growl into my breast, he pops them off, not bothering to be gentle or careful, and I can't bring myself to care.

"How wet are you for me, my Willow? How wet is this pretty cunt going to be for me?"

I make a noise that's pure nonsense in reply, and he laughs as he kisses down my stomach.

"I'm going to feast on this perfect cunt, do you understand?"

"Goddess, please, yes, that's what I want."

"You are going to take my knot tonight, Willow. I'm going to swell inside you while you come around me again and again, milking me like a good little mate, taking all my seed."

My eyes fly open in surprise, because I'm not sure what that is.

"You didn't think I'd be like the humans you've bedded, did you?" His laugh is harsh, but his hands are gentle and his eyes are full of love. Adoration. "You are so beautiful. Here." He takes my hand, pressing it against the hard bulge in his trousers.

He hisses through his teeth as I stroke the length of him, so hard and hot that a fresh wave of moisture seeps between my thighs.

"I'm wet for you, Kieran," I murmur, so in love with the way he looks at me like my touch might kill him.

His hand still covers mine, so large in comparison, and he pumps our hands over his shaft. "Right there, Willow, that's where my knot will be, and you'll be locked to me until it deflates. I'll get you ready, pretty little green witch."

I suck in a breath as he rips my pants down my legs, taking my underwear with them. He pushes my knees apart, rising up slightly and pressing my back to the bed.

"Fucking perfect."

I moan as he drags a finger through my slit, stopping just short of where I need him most.

"You're going to feel so good while you're caught on my cock and knot, Willow."

My legs begin to shake as he kisses down my calf, nipping at my knee as he continues to work his fingers so, so carefully through my sex. By the time his mouth finally reaches my cunt, I'm breathing as though I've run the length of Wild Oak Woods.

His eyes are full of triumph, and he holds my gaze as he lifts his glistening fingers to his mouth, licking them clean.

"Oh," I breathe.

"Oh," he agrees. "Never tasted anything as sweet as my mate."

Quicker than a flash, he buries his head between my thick thighs.

I reach down and grab the first thing I can, the horns protruding from his head. They're velvety soft and he groans, redoubling his efforts on the bud of my pleasure.

"Oh, goddess," I moan, my hips meeting the pace of his tongue as I hold him.

"That's right, ride my mouth," he mutters in between licks, talking me through it, each word and touch taking me higher and higher.

Two fingers nudge at my entrance as he sucks, hard, then curls his fingers slightly inside me—and I explode.

The vining plant in the corner bursts into bloom, the honeyed fragrance of jasmine filling the room after the wave of magic I released when I came.

"That's my mate," he says with a lazy grin, reaching up with one hand to fondle a breast. "I fucking love the noises you make when you come."

I shove him back, and he staggers as I tug at his clothes. "Off. Take it off. Now."

Laughing, he does as I demand, pulling off his trousers and shirt until he stands gloriously nude in front of me.

"Your body is art. The goddesses broke the mold when they made you," I tell him, and I mean every word.

He shivers as I press my mouth against his chest, tracing the cut lines of his muscles. When I glance up at him, I can't help but laugh at the tight, strained expression on his face.

"Don't laugh," he growls, hands fisting at his sides.

"I'll laugh if I want to," I tell him with an arched brow. Daring him. To do what, I don't know. "It's my turn."

I push him slightly, nudging him back to my bed, because there's no way I can do what I want with him standing, unless I want to pull a muscle in my neck or something.

Just because I have a lotion for a strained muscle doesn't mean I want to have one.

He finally sits on my bed, chest heaving, and I just watch him.

"I like you like this."

"Naked and ready to do your bidding, witch?"

I toss my hair, earning a smile from him. "Exactly."

"Are you going to force me to come with your stare alone?" he growls.

"Do you think you could?" I ask, slightly distracted by that notion.

His cock jerks, and my attention immediately refocuses.

It's my turn to drop to my knees, and I do so slowly, ready to worship at the altar of my fae prince.

I take him into my mouth slowly, adjusting to the feel of him, the girth of it.

I love it, love the sounds he's making, the way his hands scrabble for purchase on my bedding. The taste of honey and blueberries explodes across my tongue, making my eyes widen. I pull away from him, watching precum leak from the swollen tip of his cock.

Curious, I lap at it while I pump my hand up and down it, and sure enough... honey and blueberries.

Honey-and-blueberry-flavored cum. Wren's been keeping secrets.

I smile wryly before taking him deep in my mouth, making him grunt.

Can't say I blame her—I'm not sure how I would have taken that particular tidbit of information.

"You're making me so fucking ready for you. I need you. I need to knot you, mate."

"Then do something about it," I tell him sassily, then go right back to work on that delicious treat of a dick.

I squeal as he picks me up, tossing me on the bed and lining his dick up with my entrance.

"You're even wetter for me now," he marvels, and we both groan as he rubs the head of his cock against my clit. "You're going to take my knot so good, Willow."

I bare my teeth at him, sick of the teasing, and dig my nails into his hips, pulling down on him.

"Is that what you want, my soft little witch? You want me inside?"

"Now."

"Ask nicely."

"Fuck me hard, right now," I say through clenched teeth.

He hisses again as I throw my legs around his waist, driving up and onto him.

"Fuck, Willow, that's it."

He slams down into me and I cry out, seeing stars.

Full. So full. So good.

We find a rhythm quickly, my hips rising to meet his as he slams into me, coming more and more unbound with every slick slide of our bodies against one another.

He shudders, and I moan as he slides his fingers to my clit again, teasing it, making me more slippery. I'm clenching around him, desperate to come again, needing him so badly, needing something I can't describe.

"Take it, Willow," he grinds out, and my eyes fly all the way open in surprise.

He wasn't all the way in—and now there's something thick and bulging and swollen pressing into me.

"Fuck," I moan, caught between pain and pleasure.

Kieran drops his head, taking my nipple in his mouth, his fingers still rubbing my clit as his knot sinks further into me, stretching me.

"Don't rush it, Willow," he snarls as I try to aid the process by shoving into him. "Take it slow."

"I want it. Give it to me," I demand, practically snarling.

"Fuck, woman," he says in a low voice, gritting his teeth.

"That's the idea, Kieran," I say, whipping my hips up as hard as I can.

I cry out as he fills me, and he sucks in a harsh breath, swearing in a language I've never heard before.

Big hands cradle my back and my ass.

"You take me so fucking well, Willow. Look. Look at where we're bound, like mates should be." His voice is a harsh rasp against my neck, and the sharp points of his canines scrape the sensitive skin there.

I'm sensitive everywhere, all at once. Every single nerve in my body seems to be firing all at once, and it's too much.

"You can do this, love, you were made for me," Kieran says.

"It's too much," I whimper, riding the knife's edge between pleasure and pain.

"Let me help you. Tell me I can help you."

I don't know what he means and I don't care, all I know is that if something doesn't change quickly, I'm going to be more sore than that time I tried to ride a donkey who didn't want to be ridden.

"Please, yes. Do it." I nod, my entire body trembling, so grateful his muscled arms are holding me in place.

Sharp points prick into my skin and I suck in a shocked breath, a scream climbing up my throat...

He bit me—

The scream dies before it escapes.

He bit me, and oh my goddess, why didn't he bite me before now?

All rational thought completely dissolves as molten heat moves through my entire body, the deepest orgasm I've ever felt leaving me shaking in the aftershocks.

His wings beat effortlessly behind him, casting color all over my room, and he somehow moves deeper within me.

We're levitating from the bed, and even as the thought flits through my mind, another orgasm begins to build. His long fingers continue to gently stroke me, his knot fully embedded within me.

I've never felt so close to anyone, never been so fully melded in body and spirit, and emotion rocks me to the very core.

The moment he comes is like an eruption, his hot seed spurting so deep inside.

And we're not even near done, if what he said about his knot is true.

I have a feeling it is.

"Kiss me," I murmur, desperate to feel his mouth on mine.

"I love you," he tells me instead, his light eyes so full of adoration that I reach for his face, cupping it in my hands as he holds our bodies together in the air above my bed. "Forgive me for taking so long to tell you that."

I hiccup a laugh, near tears and overwhelmed with both sensation and emotion. "You could ask anything of me right now and I would give it to you," I tell him through a teary smile.

He practically preens at the praise, but then fixes me with a serious look. "That doesn't mean this conversation is over."

"It is for now," I say, finally pulling his stubborn, gorgeous face to mine and kissing him like my life depends on it.

"Are you sure?" he asks with a wry smile. "Because we're going to be stuck in bed like this for quite a while."

"I can think of other things I'd rather do and talk about than your guilt right now."

"Oh, is that right?"

"Yes," I say primly. "For starters, you could bite me again. I wouldn't mind another orgasm."

"You are a greedy mate," he tells me, slapping my ass with one hand, then jiggling it while I laugh.

"Are you complaining?" I say, nibbling at his chest.

"I am stubborn, not stupid," he huffs, then drops his mouth to my neck.

It might just be the best night of my life.

When his fangs send fresh pleasure storming through me, I decide it's definitely the best night of my life.

EPILOGUE

WILLOW

Four days.

We've been snowed in for four days—and I can't remember a time in my life I've ever been happier. Ever.

We've had a lot of sex. I'm pretty sure my room reeks of it, and I'm not ashamed, not one bit.

But more than that, we've talked. About everything and nothing, his childhood and mine, our hopes and dreams, the most embarrassing things either of us have ever done, worst choices, worst lovers... we've covered it all, until we were hoarse and thirsty.

Though the thirst might also be due to physical exertion.

Who could say?

I could happily stay indoors like this, with him, for another week. Just us, in our little snow-globe cozy cottage.

Chirp, however, is fully sick of being indoors, so on the fifth day, I manage to throw a door open.

"It looks so different," Kieran marvels, staring out at the white-cloaked world with wide eyes.

"Doesn't it?" I poke him in the side as Chirp glides away into the woods beyond the greenhouse.

He doesn't respond, and I turn my gaze slowly towards him.

"You've never seen snow," I finally say, realizing what has him stunned. "Come on," I announce, shutting the door and grabbing him by the wrist. "Let's get you dressed. We're going out to explore."

He follows without argument, letting me fuss over him as I try to find something, anything, that will keep him as warm as possible.

I like fussing over him.

I don't think he's ever had anyone truly care about him. His friends Ga'Rek and Caelan do, in their own ways, but from everything he's told me, him being royalty and, well, the spawn of the Unseelie queen didn't necessarily lead to the most healthy of friendships.

I think I'll make it part of my mission in life to do all the fussing he's missed out on.

"You sure you won't be too cold?" he asks, voice muffled by the huge banket I wound around his neck and shoulders in an incredibly oversized approximation of a scarf.

"I am built for the cold," I tell him, slapping my own ass through my thick wool coat.

"No, you're built for me," he says seriously. "Perfect for holding tight, perfect for making love to all night… and most of the day."

"Stop it," I squeal as he reaches for my breasts. "We are getting out of the house today. We have snow-day things to do."

"Like get cold?"

I raise an eyebrow at him as I tug my thickest dragon scale gloves on. "But think of how nicely we can warm up together," I say.

"In that case—" Kieran scoops me up into his arms, stomping

back to the front door and carrying me over the threshold into the snow.

"Oh," I say excitedly. "I bet Piper is open. Let's go get hot chocolate and breakfast."

"What my mate wants, my mate gets," he tells me, planting a huge, sloppy kiss on my lips, making me laugh even harder.

"You are not going to carry me the whole way."

"I will."

"No, you will not."

"I want to. Besides, you're warm. It's for my comfort."

"Well, in that case," I say, snuggling into him. "I suppose I will tolerate it."

"What's going on here?" he asks a moment later, frowning.

I follow the direction of his gaze.

A crowd of people and creatures stand around on the street, talking in loud voices and pointing.

"Is that…" I start.

"That wasn't there before," Kieran confirms. He sets me on my feet and we both scramble through the thick snow, hand in hand, to inspect the building that's somehow appeared where there was nothing but grass and air.

A heavy iron and glass-paned door anchors the building, and arched windows are covered in brown butcher paper on the inside.

It rises three stories, and I shield my eyes as I gaze up at it.

"Opening soon," Kieran reads off a red banner in front of the shop.

"How did it get here?" the harpy in front of me asks in a hushed tone, directing the question at no one and everyone all at once.

A cloaked woman turns towards us, lowering her thick velvet hood as she makes eye contact with me. Familiar near-black hair spills down her shoulder, and she purses her lips.

I nod, already knowing what she's going to say.

"They're here. It's only a matter of time until we're forced to hold up our end of a bargain we never agreed to."

Kieran squeezes my hand, and Nerissa pulls her hood back over her head, walking to the ominous front door.

I gasp as the door opens before she even touches the handle, and when she walks through it, I try to wade through the snow faster, but it's too thick.

It's too thick, and the door is closing.

I slam my hand against it, calling her name.

It's locked up tight. Even my best unlocking charm fails, though I didn't expect it to work.

Nerissa is gone.

A wolf howls mournfully in the near distance, sending a fresh chill down my spine.

"What just happened?" Kieran asks, looking as stunned as I feel.

"Nerissa's decided to take her fate into her own hands."

He tilts his head, giving me a questioning look, but I shake mine because I don't have answers, not for either of us.

I blow out a cloudy breath.

"To The Pixie's Perch," I tell him. "I have a feeling more happened over the past few days than, ah—" I feel heat spread across my cheeks, and a shy smile tugs at my lips, in spite of everything. "Than what we did," I finally finish.

"You're not worried?" he asks, narrowing his eyes at me. We both ignore the hubbub around us.

I cast a long look back at the new building. "I am."

"But?"

"She made a choice, of her own free will. Whatever she's walked into, she did so on her own terms." I chew my lip. "Piper and the rest of the witches will know more."

"And they have hot chocolate," he agrees.

"That is also important. Not as important as Nerissa getting locked in there with…" I wave a hand, still confused about whatever the hell the Elder Gods actually are. "But we can't control her, no more than whoever magicked that place into town can. I'm sure he'll find that out very, very, soon."

The words leave my mouth, and I can feel the truth of them.

Nerissa is more than capable of managing whatever is on the other side of that door.

I'm as sure of it as I am of the fae prince walking by my side.

If I'm wrong, though? I have nothing but faith in my coven—and a newfound faith in my own place in it.

GET ready for the next set of books in this world! The duchess, Nerissa, and one other witch will have their tales told in WILDER OAK WOODS, coming soon.

Subscribe to my newsletter for all the latest news on the Wild Oak Woods coven and other releases!

Afterword

If you enjoyed this book, it would mean the world to me if you'd take the time to leave a review! Reviews and readers are the lifeblood of indie authors like me, and I cannot thank you enough for taking the time to read my work!

All the love,
January

Also by January Bell

Fantasy Titles:

Wild Oak Woods World:

How To Tame A Trickster Fae
How To Woo A Warrior Orc
How To Please A Princely Fae

A Conqueror's Kingdom

Of Sword & Silver
Of Gods & Gold

Fated By Starlight

Following Fate: Prequel Novella
Claimed By The Lion: Book One
Stolen By The Scorpio: Book Two
Taurus Untamed: Book Three

Science Fiction Titles:

Accidental Alien Brides

Wed To The Alien Warlord
Wed To The Alien Prince

Wed To The Alien Brute
Wed To The Alien Gladiator
Wed To The Alien Beast
Wed To The Alien Assassin
Wed To The Alien Rogue

BOUND BY FIRE

Alien On Fire
Alien in Flames

ALIEN DATING GAMES

Alien Tides

About the Author

January Bell writes steamy fantasy and sci-fi romance with a guaranteed happily ever after. Combining pure escapism, a little adventure, and a whole lotta love makes for romance that's a world apart. January spends her days writing, herding kids and ducks, and spends the nights staring at the stars.

For the latest updates, sign up for my newsletter by visiting www.januarybellromance.com, or follow me on Instagram and TikTok.

DEEP IN THE WINTER WOODS

PIPER & GA'REK BONUS SCENE

DEEP IN THE WINTER WOODS

PIPER

Chaos seems to have taken control of every aspect of my otherwise very orderly life.

Wild magic surrounding our perfect hamlet? Yes.

Ancient magic elementals threatening my coven? Yes.

Massive early winter storm threatening? You guessed it!

The ginger and cranberry cake in the oven refusing to take my energy spell? Also yes.

Sighing, I lean heavily against the kitchen counter and rub my temples.

"So stressed, my little éclair?" Ga'Rek's voice rumbles in my ear, and then his big hands masterfully massage my shoulders.

I groan as he hits a particularly stubborn knot, melting against his broad chest.

"You don't need to worry about the cake, my sweet. Most of the town is planning to stay inside for this storm."

"I don't understand why the ginger cake won't accept the charm," I almost whine the words, pressing my forehead against his body.

"Then let it be what it wants. Even a cake that's unspelled from your kitchen will be more delicious than anyone else's."

I smile into his chest, then peek up at him as he continues rubbing my shoulders.

"You always know what to say."

"It's easy to do when it's the truth."

Sighing happily, I wrap my arms around the big orc, soaking in both his warmth and the heat of the oven behind me. Ginger and sugar and butter and cinnamon pervades the air in a heady aroma.

"It does smell good," I admit.

"You smell good," he tells me, the words taking on a growly undertone that turns my legs to jelly.

The gnomish brass mechanical timer dings on the counter, and Ga'Rek releases me from his embrace so I can pull the heavy gingerbread cake from the oven.

I've used my heatproofing spell, which took me a whole year to master, but enables me to use my bare hands. Wonderful for days I'm baking heavily. I have a tendency to misplace my dragonskin gloves nearly constantly.

"I don't think I'll ever not panic when I see you reach in the oven like that," Ga'Rek tells me, hovering behind my shoulders like an overprotective hen as I set the cake on a wire rack. "I thought you only used that spell on our busy days."

I frown, because I'm not sure why I used the spell.

"You must be stressed if you wanted to work that magic anyway." His lips brush over the nape of my neck, his hands on my waist. "You can't shoulder the responsibility for what's happening."

"I know that," I say, feeling stubborn and tired all at once.

"But you want to anyway, don't you, Piper?" He spins me around slowly, forcing me to meet his knowing gaze.

He's breathtaking. I should be used to his size by now, the

aggressively masculine features, the tusks that gleam in the soft evening light.

Instead, I stare up at him with all the love and admiration that a male like my mate deserves.

He presses his mouth to mine, and I moan as the kiss deepens, the stress starting to slowly melt away.

"I have a surprise for you," he says, leaving me leaning against him after he's effectively turned me to a molten mess.

"Oh. Molten mess might be a good name for the fudge cakes with gooey centers I've been working on," I say.

He chuckles softly, another kiss landing on my forehead. "Always thinking so hard."

"A surprise?" I repeat, finally realizing what he's said.

"Aye, my love," he tells me, grinning. "Something to take your mind off everything. You deserve to relax, Piper."

I nibble at my lower lip, looking up at him through my lashes.

"I don't even have to ask what you're thinking. I know it's hard for you to let things go, but Piper, even in times like these, you have to take care of yourself. And if you aren't able to, you will let me."

"I like surprises," I tell him. "Good surprises, at least."

His hands go to the counter behind me, and I love the way he's caged me in. "This will be a good surprise. You'll have to leave the cake behind, though."

"Let me at least turn it out before it sticks to the pan," I tell him with a laugh, shoving his chest lightly.

"As if any of your cakes ever stick to the pan."

"There's a first time for everything," I say reproachfully. He's not wrong, though. The spell I use to keep baked goods from sticking works well.

A little too well, considering how I've sent more cookies flying from the pans when I went I took a spatula to them.

He continues to nuzzle my neck as I work on the cake. I slide a wooden spatula I designed specifically for this purpose around the rim of the bundt cake.

I frown, because sure enough, the damned cake is sticking.

"The spell didn't work."

He pauses, breath ghosting along my shoulder as he looks at what I'm doing. "And you said the other spell didn't take?"

I blow a frustrated breath out. "Right…" a thought occurs to me. "I wonder if the ginger and cranberry combination have some sort of spell resistance."

"It's a new recipe, right?"

"It is." I stick my tongue out as I concentrate on every so carefully working the cake away from the edges, then press a second wire rack against the top and flip the whole thing.

It begins to come out of the pan, and I hold my breath… only to wince as the top third sticks.

"I think your theory is a good one," he says, clearly shocked by the cake's imperfection.

"About spell resistance?"

"Aye." His green hand snakes out before I can slap it away and he grabs a huge chunk of still steaming cake, popping it in his mouth.

An unholy noise follows, and I wait for his verdict.

His fingers dig into my sides. "Fucking delicious," he finally pronounces around the cake. More steam comes from his mouth, and I let out a laugh, bopping him on the nose.

"You look like a dragon."

"Everyone knows dragons aren't real." His throat bobs as he swallows. "But if they were, I'm pretty sure all you'd have to do is feed them this cake to tame them, spelled or not."

Hmm. "I'll have to ask Willow about a ginger and cranberry combination effect."

I take a smaller bit of the disaster cake from inside the pan. My eyes widen in surprise as it hits my tongue.

Ga'Rek isn't just being kind.

The cake is delicious, with or without any type of charm on it.

"Maybe I could try to spell it once it's baked," I muse.

"Enough," Ga'Rek tells me quietly, though there's a note of no-nonsense command in it that makes me arch my eyebrows in surprise.

"I like surprises, but Ga'Rek, you can't just expect me to put everything I'm worried about aside—" I start.

He presses a finger to my mouth, and I open my mouth and bite down on it in annoyance.

Which only succeeds in making him laugh. The sound is contagious, and it's not long before I'm laughing with him.

"You really think those blunt little teeth of yours are going to hurt me?" he asks. He raises my hand to his mouth and grazes his tusks against my knuckles.

Before I realize he's distracting me, he grabs another hunk of cake with his spare hand and pops it in his mouth.

This time, I laugh immediately, giving up.

He sober as he chews, though, his finger gently stroking my hair.

"Even when it feels like the world is falling apart, you have to take care of yourself, Piper. It's more important in those moments than ever. If you fall apart, how will I put the world back together?"

My heart expands, and my eyes sting with sudden tears.

I press onto the balls of my feet, pulling my mouth to his. We kiss for a long moment, a familiar, pleasant tension growing with every passing second.

He lets out a growl, then swings me up into his arms, making me squeal. The sound quickly turns into laughter as he steals another hunk of my ginger and cranberry cake disaster, then storms up the stairs to our home, taking them two at a time while I laugh and laugh.

The door creaks open, and my laughter dies on my lips.

My jaw drops, and I have to remember to breathe as I soak in what I'm seeing.

Our humble home has been transformed.

No more is the snug kitchen, the cozy den, or the hall that leads to bedrooms.

Snow falls from the vaulted ceiling, the chandelier that hangs overhead draped in greenery as the candles cast a soft glow on… the winter woods.

"I wanted to give you something you'd never forget. A night in the woods, spent with me keeping you warm, without any of the dirt or discomfort that involves." He chuckles at the slack-jawed expression on my face. "Nerissa enchanted it. Took her half the day."

I inhale, and sure enough, the subtle tinge of Nerissa's magic is there, powerful, but in this instance, soothing and calm.

"She worked a relaxation spell."

Ga'Rek shifts uncomfortably at my announcement. "I did pay her extra for that, aye. I thought you could use it. Are you mad?"

I shake my head, because by the goddess, I feel better just having breathed it in. My muscles all relax at once.

"It's an illusion?" I can't quite believe it, even though the snow falling from the ceiling drifts right through my hand, not cold at all.

The place where my hearth normally is looks like a crackling campfire, complete with a stew bubbling happily atop the flames.

"It is." He sounds uncertain, and as he sets me down, he rubs the back of his neck.

I throw my arms around his neck. "It's a beautiful surprise."

"For my beautiful mate, this is the least I could do. Now," he says, arching an eyebrow and tilting his head. "You're mine for the rest of the night, and likely until this winter storm blows over. The illusion will last until tomorrow night, and I have some ideas about how we can pretend everything else doesn't exist."

I raise my own eyebrows, giving him a sly smile. "Oh? I can't imagine what that would be."

Growling, he starts to tug at my clothes, peppering kisses across every inch of exposed skin as he goes.

Ga'Rek's right— he knows exactly how to make me forget the rest of the world exists, no illusion magic needed.

He's enough, all on his own.

Printed in Great Britain
by Amazon